Holidate
PURSUIT
- A HOLIDAY NOVELLA -

BETHANY ROSA

GALLATIN PUBLISHING

Holidate Pursuit
Published by Gallatin Publishing

Copyright © 2024 by Bethany Rosa all rights reserved.

No part of this book may be reproduced in any form or by any mechanical means, including information storage and retrieval systems without permission in writing from the publisher/author, except by a reviewer who may quote passages in a review.

All images, logos, quotes, and trademarks included in this book are subject to use according to trademark and copyright laws of the United States of America.

ISBN: 979-8-9895732-4-0

Romance / Contemporary

Cover design by Jolene Morice, copyright owned by Bethany Rosa.

This is a work of fiction. Names, characters, businesses, places, events and incidents are either the products of the author's imagination or used in a fictitious manner. Any resemblance to actual persons, living or dead, or actual events is purely coincidental.

All rights reserved by Bethany Rosa and Gallatin Publishing.

Gallatin Publishing

THE *pursuit* SERIES

Pursuit of Innocence

Holidate Pursuit

Dangerous Pursuit

Pursuit of Love (mid-2025)

Did you miss Sebastian and Lily's story in
Pursuit of Innocence?

"I'm done waiting around. You're mine. No more games or pining over someone else when it's me you want. You won't remember his name after I get through with you."

Lily knows exactly what she wants in life. To graduate, land a high-paying job, and forge her own way. Nothing will distract her. Until the ultimate playboy, billionaire Sebastian Dubree, barges in. Not to be overlooked, Lily's longtime crush, Jackson, decides she's worth the fight.

Reluctant to succumb to either, she quickly becomes a challenge to conquer. Lily must decide between the familiarity of her childhood longing or the newly discovered passion ignited by the dominant CEO. But can she surrender without losing herself in the process, or will someone take matters into his own hands?

Boundaries blur between desire and resistance in this gripping coming-of-age romance, leaving readers yearning for more.

Visit www.bethanyrosa.com to explore other books in
The Pursuit Series

Or scan the link below:

Holidate

PURSUIT

- A HOLIDAY NOVELLA -

Prologue

Lucy

ALL I CAN THINK AS ELI WALKS DOWN THE HALL TOWARD my desk is thank God I don't have a crush on him anymore. After seeing Justin for the past couple of weeks, I've finally been freed of the infatuation I've had with my boss's brother, who happens to have an office down the hall from my desk. In fact, after Justin rocked my world on Friday, I've forgotten why I was ever attracted to Eli in the first place.

It was ah-mazing. First, we went to dinner at a new Italian restaurant he remembered I'd wanted to try before ending up at my place. It was our fifth date, and I'd already decided that if Justin made the first move, I was more than ready to go further—as in, let's get it on.

The guy is a walking wet dream, for starters. Add in his profession… He's a hired hitman—just kidding, he's not. But he is a bodyguard, which is how we met. My boss hired him to protect his girlfriend. Okay, it was more like spy on her, but hey, I'd let Justin spy on me any day.

Anyway, the first time he came into the office, he was all sexy and sly, flattering me like I'd never been before. It surprised me because that kind of thing doesn't usually happen to me. I mean, here's this sex on a stick standing in front of me with a shaved head—I'm a sucker for that—muscles for miles, and a rigidness about him that does nothing but make me want to see what it would take to loosen him up.

I'm usually standoffish, more of the look-and-keep-going type, but when he was at my desk for an appointment with my boss, there was simply nowhere to go. In the end, I gave him my number since he made it clear he wasn't leaving without it. Little did he know, I wouldn't have let him. My usual reluctance just wasn't there.

After calling me that same afternoon to say he couldn't wait a second longer to hear my voice again, we went out the following night. Ladies and gentlemen, it may have been lust at first sight, but that's nothing compared to love at first date. I could have stared into his beautiful brown eyes all night while listening to his slightly Southern drawl. Unfortunately, our date came to an end when we were asked to leave at closing. The sweet kiss he gave me before helping me into the Uber confirmed I'd found a true gentleman until Friday night—when one night between the sheets with Justin ruined me for all others.

Jarring me from my thoughts, Eli stops at my desk. "Morning, Lucy. I wanted to let you know that Sebastian won't be in for a couple of days."

"Is he sick?" That's the only thing that would keep him from the office.

"No. I wish that were the reason. Lily had an incident this weekend. She was kidnapped from the gala on Friday—"

"Oh my God, is she okay? What happened?" I like Mr. Dubree's girlfriend, Lily. It's weird saying that since, one—I didn't think he would ever have a girlfriend—and two, certainly not one I'd like.

"She is. Some psycho friend from school was obsessed with her and thought taking her was the way to get noticed. Luckily, Sebastian got there before anything major happened, but she was pretty shaken up. Sebastian certainly was. She's safe and recuperating at his place. They'll probably surface by Wednesday or Thursday, but I'll keep you posted. In the meantime, let me know if you need anything."

"I will. Tell Mr. Dubree I'm sorry and let them know they're in my thoughts."

"Sure. Thanks, Lucy." He walks off toward his office, leaving me in shock.

That's unbelievable… the kind of thing you hear about in movies or true crime shows, not in real life. Geez.

Maybe that's why I haven't heard from Justin since he left Saturday morning. We had just finished breakfast after round three, or maybe it was four—yeah, it was definitely four—when his phone rang. After a quick kiss when the call ended, he left for an emergency at work. His parting words were, "I'm so sorry, babe. Hate to run off like this, but I'll call you later," and then he was out the door.

There was no call later, and when I didn't get a response to my text yesterday, I told myself he was just busy and tried not to let it go to my head. I'll admit that my mind started going a little crazy this morning, so the new information is helpful. With Justin being Mr. Dubree's security officer, he's probably up to his eyeballs with paperwork, details, and whatever else Mr. Dubree has him doing after a scare like that. I'm sure he'll call soon.

I'm anxious while heading into work this morning, knowing Mr. Dubree is back. I'm sure he'll already be in since he usually gets here at the crack of dawn. Although maybe that will change now that he and Lily patched things up after their hiatus. According to Eli, she's been at his place the last few days. Maybe he'll turn over a new leaf and not work so much. However, I hope that's not the case today because I'm dying to ask him about Justin.

It's been four days since I've heard from him, and I'm eager to get any information I can from Mr. Dubree. Waiting for his return to bring it up has been torturous. The problem is, I'll have to be sly about it. It's not like I told my boss that I was sleeping with the head of his security team. However, I did accidentally call Justin by his first name once and may have blown my cover anyway. Oh well, it's not like there's any rule against interoffice dating, and even if there were, does a subcontractor count?

I'll be finding out soon because, sure enough, he's in his office when I reach my desk. Putting my things down, I inhale slowly to calm myself, grab a pen and notepad, and head in.

"Good morning, Mr. Dubree. I'm so sorry to hear about what happened to Lily over the weekend. Thank goodness you got there in time. Is she doing okay?" He looks up from his computer and sets his pen down to respond.

"Thank you, Lucy. Yes, she's doing much better. It'll take some time for her to feel safe after the whole fiasco, but I'm doing everything I can to ensure she is. I'm just thankful the situation was contained before more damage was done."

"Me too. I'm sure it helped that you already had security in place, right?" This is the opening I was hoping for.

"It did and didn't. Unfortunately, I'd let security go for the evening after she was safely inside. My concern was for reporters, not a stalker. On the other hand, I was lucky Mr. Burns investigated the guy on a hunch and already had his address. I only wish I'd had the information earlier." He sighs and runs his hand through his hair in frustration.

Here's my opportunity. "I'm glad Mr. Burns was able to help. Will he be protecting Lily full-time from now on?" That might explain why he's been too busy to call.

"She will be under protection 24/7 moving forward—you can count on that—but Mr. Burns has selected two of his own from Southpaw Security to be employed directly by me. I'll email you their information so you know who they are. Interrupt me anytime they call, no matter what meeting I'm in."

"Certainly, sir. So, we won't be dealing with Mr. Burns anymore?" *That was subtle, right?*

"Not on a daily basis. However, I'll still use his company and services for investigative work, such as background checks. So, tell me, are there any pressing issues I need to address from the last few days before moving forward?"

"Oh, right. Uh… no, not really. You'll see a daily rundown in your inbox. Let me know if you have any questions. Otherwise, things went smoothly while you were out, and Eli handled anything that needed immediate attention, sir."

"Great. I'll let you know if I need anything else. Thank you, Lucy."

"Good to have you back, sir," I say, shutting the door behind me.

I'm numb while staring at my computer, at a total loss for what to do next. After the best night of my life—what *appeared* to be the best night for both of us—he vanished without a trace. Was it all an act? Was I dreadful in bed? I mean, yes, he was way more experienced, but he seemed just as enthusiastic, not to mention equally satisfied.

So now what? I don't want to be that psycho who, after one night together, becomes obsessed with the guy, but dammit, I thought we had a connection beyond that. It's possible he's too busy handling the employee transfers and hasn't had time to reach out. Oh God, I'm delusional if that's what I'm telling myself. It takes seconds to send a text and five minutes for a phone call—hell, I'd take one minute at this point.

Still, the question remains… what should I do? The last text I sent was Monday after hearing what happened to let him know I was thinking about him and hoped he was okay. *Missing you. Hope to hear from you soon!* were my last words. It was too needy, I bet. Damn, this sucks.

I'm not sure if I should try to send another text or just pick up the phone and call. Dang it, I liked this guy. I wouldn't have screwed him until I could barely walk if I didn't. The fact that it took five dates to do it is wild, considering I was ready after the third. He was a perfect gentleman, though, and at the end of each, he would kiss me and send me home alone. I started to get worried that he wasn't sexually attracted to me until his texts became flirty, setting the stage for more. Then, finally, on date number four, he gave me the most panty-melting kiss that seemed to go on forever yet was still too short. If both Ubers weren't already on their way, our next stop would've been my place.

As it was, we couldn't have connected any better or progressed more perfectly. After he left that morning, I even thought he could be the one. And now, here we are. The more I deliberate, the more irritated I get, so I decide to send one more text and leave the ball in his court.

> Me: Hey, it sounds like you've been busy with everything. Shoot me a quick text if you have time, just to let me know you're okay. Thinking of you.

The weekend comes and goes, and I don't hear a word from the bastard. How could I be so naïve? My anguish has turned to anger, and my pride is too hurt to let it go, so I put the nail in the coffin with one final text.

> Me: At this point, you've made it clear I was nothing but a notch on your bedpost. Too bad you wasted your money on two extra dates since you could've made it sooner.

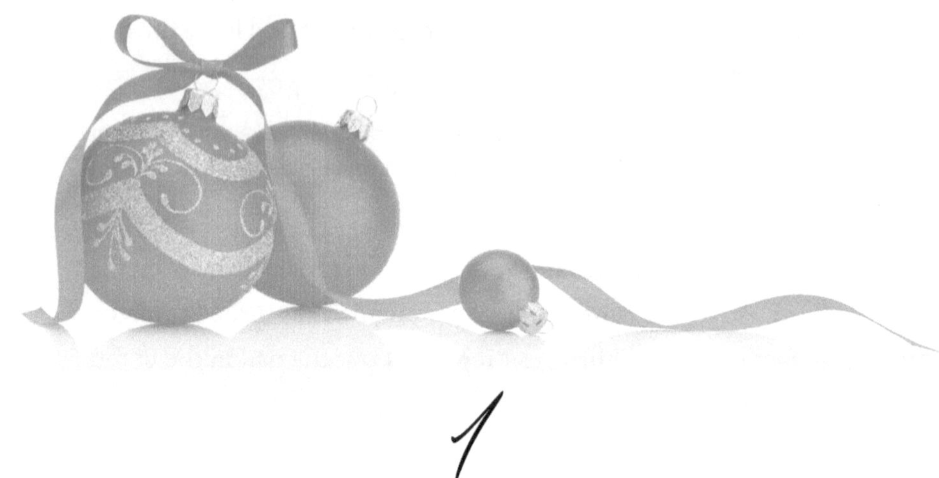

1

PRE-SEASON MISCHIEF

"Y OU SHOULD'VE LET ME SET YOU UP WITH JORDAN FROM marketing. He's cute, and you need to date more. You're not getting any younger, you know," Lily says above the pounding music of the club while nudging me with a smirk.

"Whatever, Mom. Twenty-six is not the age to start worrying," I say, rolling my eyes and sipping my drink.

"Did I just hear that correctly? It sounded like my fiancé just said her coworker was cute. I'm sure I must be mistaken. It is quite loud in here." Sebastian—as he insists I call him when we're outside of the office—butts in while putting his finger in his ear and wiggling it.

Lily leans over and places her hand on his chest while batting her eyes at him. "We almost had something before you came in like a caveman, you know."

I swear she gives me a heart attack every time I'm out with the two of them, constantly pushing his buttons. As I've been working for Sebastian this long, I know his buttons are not ones you should push. She's the only one who can manage it unscathed.

"Lily, if you talk about having anything with another man again, you'll regret it," Sebastian says in his authoritative tone that anyone who knows him fears—except Lily.

"Sebastian, you do realize you weren't the first—" She squeals as he lifts her mid-sentence and tosses her over his shoulder, giving a swat to her ass as he carries her off, probably headed to Sebastian's back office since he and Eli own the place.

Because we've become such good friends over the past few months, I know Lily goaded him on purpose. It's funny to watch, but it also causes a slight amount of jealousy to sneak up. Almost having that connection with someone not so long ago makes it difficult to see. I've yet to put myself back out there—and it's been six months. I'm not a total recluse, but it affected me more than I expected.

"I'm sure they'll be gone awhile, and I'm headed to the bar. Do you want me to grab you another drink?" Eli asks as he rises from his seat.

"That'd be great. I'll take a prosecco."

He nods to security as he walks away, indicating they should move closer to the table while I'm alone. The Dubrees have had constant security in place ever since Lily's kidnapping. It was weird to get used to when Lily and I started hanging out, but it doesn't bother me anymore. It's barely noticeable other than constantly reminding me of the one that got away. Or should I say ran away?

"Are you having fun tonight, ma'am?" the guard asks. Tom, I think his name is.

"You did not just call me ma'am. I mean, you're like, what… twenty-nine? Thirty? I'm younger than you." Do I look like a ma'am? I was going for more of a hottie vibe. Dammit.

He holds his hands up in defense. "Whoa, I didn't mean to offend you. The term has more to do with respect than age." He holds his hand out. "I'm Tom. You're Lucy, right?"

Well, now I feel bad. "Yeah. And sorry. I shouldn't have snapped at you. Maybe that answers your question—I guess I'm not having as much fun as I'd hoped." His hand is surprisingly soft for his rugged appearance.

"That's too bad. If it's any consolation, your costume's great." His eyes couldn't make it more obvious which part he thinks is great.

I look down to see my breasts pushed up from the top of my Tinker Bell costume, and I can't blame him—they do look damn good. It's the one day a year the ladies get attention thanks to the rolls of socks stuffed in my bra, which is the goal, of course—why else would I have socks anywhere other than my feet?

I smile up at him. "Thanks. Lily picked all our costumes. Speaking of, I'm not sure how Eli's going to carry both our drinks back with one hand." He got stuck being Captain Hook. I think Sebastian's more suited for the character, but with Lily being Wendy and all, that wasn't about to happen.

"He'll manage, I'm sure. So, are you two dating then?"

"Who? Me and Eli?" He nods. "God, no. He's my boss—well, technically Sebastian is, but Eli is by default." Months ago, that question would have made me turn ten shades of red since it was once a dream of mine. But after spending more time together now that Lily and I are friends, Eli and I have become friends as well.

"Does that mean you'd want to go out later?" he asks with a smirk.

"Oh… uh… I don't know…"

He raises his eyebrows in question.

"You work for the Dubrees, too, so that might be messy." Been there, done that, security guard and all.

"Good thing I like to get messy. Plus, I'm going to fantasize about being showered in your fairy dust all night," Tom says, wiggling his eyebrows as Eli appears with my drink, my mouth hanging open in shock.

"Dude. You just spewed that shit?" Eli says to him.

"Hey, just tryin' to have a little fun, is all."

"Yeah, well, get back to your job before Sebastian gets here and sees you flirting with his woman's friend."

Tom gives me a wink and a sexy smile before walking away, which isn't a minute too soon since Lily plops down next to me in the second that follows.

"Hey, what was that about? Was Tom flirting with you?" she asks immediately, seeing his departure.

"Something like that," I respond, then add, "I can't believe you just left. Scratch that—I can."

"It's not like I was given a choice."

"Riiight. You egged him on, and you know it."

"It happens to be my favorite pastime," she says with a sly smile. "Now, tell me about Tom over there. What did he say?"

Before answering, I glance over to make sure Sebastian isn't paying attention since Eli's comment made it clear that Sebastian wouldn't handle Tom's flirting very well. "He asked if I wanted to go out later," I finally respond.

"And…?"

"And nothing. I told him we work together, so…"

"So, nothing. Lucy, you need to get out there… date… have a one-night stand or something."

"Yeah, because that went so well last time."

"You know what they say, the best way to get over someone is to get under someone else. Let's go dance and see if there's anyone you can't use the work excuse with. Come on." She stands, dragging me with her.

It doesn't go unnoticed that Tom and another bodyguard follow us to the dance floor, flanking us on either side. I'm not sure how we're supposed to find anyone else with Starsky and Hutch hovering.

Maybe Lily's right and I do need a one-night stand. Tom is undoubtedly easy on the eyes and probably good in the bedroom. Damn Justin for making me question everything so much. He really did a number on me if I'm still letting his rejection affect me months later. It's just that I still don't know if it was because I lacked bedroom skills or if he pulled the wool over my eyes, and his plan all along was to one and done me.

The bottom line is this is completely ridiculous, and I need to stop thinking about him because it doesn't matter. What matters is that right here, right now, he's gone, so it's time to get my damn groove on.

"I'm glad you at least gave it a go. Sorry it didn't work out," Lily says as she fixes her coffee the next day.

Last night, after a few flirty looks from Tom on the dance floor, I decided to sample the goods. Giving my goodbyes to Lily and the others, it was no surprise when he offered to escort me to my Uber. Of course, since I'm with the owners, I use the back entrance, which was apparently private enough for a test run.

He made his move the moment we stepped outside and after being met with no resistance, he let me have it. Sure, it was hot, but the spark I was hoping for—the one to make me want to climb him like a tree then and there—was unfortunately missing. By the time he pulled away, rather than alluding to wanting more and leading him on, I graciously thanked him and said I'd see him next time, leaving him speechless as I got into the car.

"That's okay. I still had fun. And besides, you never know, right?" I shrug.

"You should still let me set you up with Jordan."

"Again, Lily, he works for the same company. It's bad enough that I'll be seeing Tom all the time."

"Yeah, but you're not even on the same floor as Jordan. And as you can see, I brought Patrick instead of Tom. I'll keep doing that when I only need one of them." She nods toward the guy near the café's entrance. Sebastian insists a guard is always with her, but for special occasions, he requires two. I'm guessing that coffee with me was small enough to warrant only one.

"Thank you, but it's still too close for comfort with Jordan. It would be uncomfortable if things ended badly, which is my track record lately. And if it did work out, then it could get awkward. It's a double-edged sword."

"Or it could be a win-win. Look at me and Sebastian, it's not awkward, and we get to see each other more."

"Totally different. He owns the fricking company and makes

the rules. Plus, you guys are engaged, not dating. And by the way? News flash—it's definitely awkward now and then. Don't think I don't know what you're doing in his office half the time. You're lucky I love you." I point my spoon at her as she guiltily looks down at her cup.

"I'm going to pretend I didn't hear that and feign ignorance. As for being engaged, we didn't start that way. We dated. Just like you need to do"—she points her spoon back at me—"to find Mr. Right. Any other excuses before I get the ball rolling?"

"Ugh. Fine. I'll go on one date," I say, rolling my eyes and shaking my head.

A smile lights up her face, and she opens her mouth to respond, but I cut her off, holding my hand up before she has a chance.

"Hang on. How do you even know he wants to take me out— have you talked to him? And why hasn't he already asked if he's so interested?" I ask suspiciously.

"Okay, I haven't actually talked to him yet, but you're both single and good-looking, so why not?" She shrugs.

"I've been arguing about a hypothetical this whole time?" I roll my eyes.

"Hey, at least I got your permission first. You're lucky I'm not Cici. That girl does what she wants, when she wants, and doesn't think about asking permission from anyone for anything. I seriously can't wait for you to meet her." She beams.

"Me too. Hopefully I'll get to before the wedding."

"I hope so too. Especially since you'll be working on the fun stuff together." She wiggles her brows.

"I wouldn't get your hopes up about the fun part. Sebastian has his own definition of fun, and I'm pretty sure he'll have a lot of say in what Cici and I put together."

"I have faith she'll get what she wants when it comes down to it."

"We'll see about that. Anyway, back to this Jordan thing, keep me posted, okay? I don't want any surprises." I give her the stink eye.

"I will. Promise. In case it leads to something, what are your plans for the holidays?"

"I'm going home. My parents allowed me to move a thousand miles away on the condition I come home for Thanksgiving and Christmas. It was a bargain, trust me," I say, taking a sip of coffee to wash down my distaste for the topic.

"Oh," she says in surprise. "I feel bad that we've never talked about your family. I'm so used to not talking about mine that I forget to ask other people about theirs. I'm sorry."

"Don't be. I prefer not to, honestly."

"Okay, spill. What's the scoop? Less than perfect parents, I'm assuming?"

"Oh no, that's the problem. They're so perfect that no one is good enough for them, and they won't be happy until I marry the perfect man, have perfect babies, and live in the perfect house on the perfect street while my perfect brother gets the moon handed to him. Get the picture?"

"Sounds perfect to me," she deadpans, causing us both to crack up.

2

GIVE THANKS

Lucy

THE DOOR TO THE TOWN CAR SWINGS OPEN, AND DARRYL, MY parents' butler, gives me a welcoming smile.

"Head on in, and I'll bring your luggage to your room. Nice to have you home, Lucy," he says, slightly bowing as he does.

"Thanks, Darryl. Not sure I can say the same, but check back in a couple of days." I smile up at him.

He chuckles knowingly. "Will do. Try to enjoy your visit, miss."

"Well, look what the cat dragged in," my brother, Trevor, calls out from the porch of the enormous Floridian beachfront mansion—my home for the first eighteen years of life.

Climbing the ridiculous ten steps to greet him, I call him out.

"All of you were too busy to come get me yourselves, huh?" I ask with a hand on my hip, cocked to the side.

"Oh, you know, Mom and Dad had an important tee time."

"Yeah? What's your excuse?"

Once I entered baggage claim, our driver was holding a sign with my name on it—a typical welcome. I'm not surprised, nor am I heartbroken, because frankly, I'm used to it.

"Well, dear sister, my excuse is I was just notified of your arrival twenty minutes ago when they texted me you'd be here soon. Now bring it in." He holds his arms open, and I curl into them. Being away from Trevor is the hardest part about living so far away. For all the coldness my parents give me, Trevor has always had a sweet spot for his little sister.

"I'm not surprised they forgot. I'm sure there are more important things to worry about, like their handicap."

"Ah, don't worry about them. You have me, and that's all you need. How about we start this visit right with a cocktail by the pool and have a real conversation before they get here?" he asks, squeezing me before letting go.

"Good idea. You need to catch me up on your latest fling anyway," I say as he leads me to the bar.

"That's a conversation not worth having."

We stay in touch, but keeping up with his dating life is hard. Everyone in our social circle tries to marry their kid to an Alcott. And since I moved away, all the attention has gone to Trevor. Between my parents and their friends, it's a wonder he's not betrothed yet. As it is, the pressure is heavy, and one of the main reasons I moved. Sorry, people—I'm not going to date your son just because he's rich and has my parents' approval.

On the other hand, Trevor is having the time of his life.

Women are lined up, a new one ready to go as soon as he's bored with the last. These poor girls have no idea it's just a game to him and that he, too, won't be surrendering to our parents' whims. They're not as intense with him though. It always made me a tad resentful that they're more lenient with Trevor, but I've finally moved past it and made peace with the fact that my parents mean well but suck at showing it.

"So, how ya been, sis?" Trevor asks as he pours two glasses of bubbly.

He insists on celebrating my annual visiting season with a bottle of the finest. No complaints here.

"Fairly good. Work is the same, though Sebastian's been more mellow ever since Lily came along. Her becoming a good friend was a surprise—a good one. She's sweet, but she's been acting like Mom lately, always trying to get me to date. She's trying to set me up with this guy from the office as we speak." I roll my eyes, taking the glass he hands me.

"Cheers to the both of us then. Single, smart, and not suicidal," he says, holding his glass up.

"Cheers."

"And speaking of smart, tell me why you're still pretending to be a secretary when you have a master's from Harvard." He leads the conversation as we walk out to the pool, the cool ocean breeze refreshing after a long day of travel.

"Don't start. I get enough of that from Mom and Dad. And I've already told you, I do it because it's easy and I like my job. I'm also paid enough to make it worth it. For all of Sebastian Dubree's faults, compensating his employees well isn't one of them."

"You're crazy, but whatever floats your boat."

"Enough about me. Where are things with Daphne?" I say, turning the tables on him.

"Nowhere. Who's this guy Lily's trying to set you up with?"

"Uh-uh, don't try to get out of it. Spill. If you're not with Daphne, who are you seeing these days, or is the infamous bachelor available?"

"I didn't say I wasn't with her, just that we've gotten nowhere. She's difficult," he says cryptically.

Now, *this* has my attention. "Difficult how?"

"She's not into it. It's obvious her parents forced her to go out with me."

"That's nothing new. What's the problem?"

"The problem is, most girls are all too eager, and she's barely giving me the time of day."

"Oh my gosh, you like her. Who are you, and what have you done with my brother?" We both laugh.

"Knock it off. I'm just being… challenged, and it's refreshing. She intrigues me, not to mention she can actually hold a conversation about real topics, like work and politics, not just bullshit. I might be interested in more with her. But as I said, we're nowhere because she's not interested."

"That's not the Trevor I know. The Trevor I know would show this girl who he is and prove to her she can't refuse. If anyone is worthy, it's you, so don't give up."

"Thanks, Luce, I won't." He looks at his watch. "We've only got about thirty minutes 'til the 'rents get here. Let's finish this bottle and hide the evidence."

"Lovely idea," I agree as we clink our glasses and bottoms up.

One more night to go. I've got this. I will survive the final dinner with my parents before returning to the land of normal. With one last look in the mirror while giving myself a pep talk, I'm prepared for my pending doom. Hopefully, Trevor's here already, or I'm going to lose it.

Before rounding the corner toward the living room, voices signal that we have guests. Good. My remaining night home might be bearable. Feeling better about the evening, I enter the room with a smile.

"Ah, there she is now," Mom says when she sees me.

There are three additional people: a couple who look to be about my parents' age and a guy who I'm assuming is their son. Perhaps a friend of Trevor's?

"Lucy, come here so I can introduce you to our friends." My mom beckons me with her hand.

Silently thanking whoever they are for joining us, I comply, smiling softly.

"Lucy, this is Mr. and Mrs. Whitehall and their son Nathan. They've recently relocated from New York, and we've been inseparable since. Nathan is also home for the holiday. He works for a company similar to yours, so I imagine you have *a lot* in common."

They shake my hand and give me their first names, insisting that's what I call them. Little do they know, I'll never remember regardless, so it's inconsequential. Once Nathan greets me and the formalities are out of the way, my goal is to ruin Mom's plan to set me up, which I'm positive she's trying to do.

"While our companies may be similar, I'm sure our positions aren't. I'm just a secretary," I point out before asking my mom, "Where is Trevor?"

Brushing my question off by telling me Trevor had other plans, she quickly returns the conversation to me. "Now, don't be modest, dear. You're the secretary to the CEO of Dubree Enterprises himself. I'm certain you wouldn't have that position if you didn't have an MBA from Harvard on your resumé," Mom purposefully brags.

"You work alongside Sebastian Dubree?" Nathan asks as if she just told him I won the Nobel Prize or something equally absurd.

Oh geez, here we go. "I wouldn't say alongside… more like way under, as in the bottom. I'm pretty much his personal lackey."

"Hell, I'd be the lackey to that man any day of the week. He's basically a god," he says, unfazed.

"Lily, his fiancé, would agree with you. On the other hand, I can attest to him being quite the tyrant." There's no need to embellish things. The worse I make it sound, the quicker this charade will end.

"I'm sure Lucy has plenty of stories to share. Don't you, sweetheart? We'll go join your dad so you two can talk." Mom ushers Nathan's parents away in the most obvious attempt possible to leave us alone.

It's not that Nathan is unattractive. On the contrary, I'd say he's handsome in a "guy your parents would approve of" sort of way. But I refuse to give in and entertain any notion of dating someone just because my parents want me to. My whole life, I've been molded into their ideal version of the perfect daughter, and when I went to college, I realized the word *perfect* just wasn't in my vocabulary.

I hate to be rude, though, so asking Nathan a question about his job seems like the polite thing to do. "So, what do you do, then? My mom mentioned we work in a similar field."

"I'm a strategist for a large investment firm in the city. New York, I mean. We're light-years behind Dubree Enterprises but sizable in the grand scheme of things. I still can't get over the fact that you work for the man himself. What's he like?" He's like a kid in a candy store.

Internally rolling my eyes, I answer and indulge in conversation until Darryl finally calls us to dinner.

Our fathers are seated at one end of the table, Nathan and I at the other, with our moms in between. My mother wastes no time. "You two seem to have a lot to talk about. You could always continue your conversation further if you'd like. Our driver can bring you somewhere for a nightcap." Here we go. She may as well bring out the prenup.

"My flight is early in the morning, so that's probably not a good idea. Sorry." *Not sorry.*

"Well, at least exchange phone numbers to stay in touch. Maybe you can get together when you both come home for Christmas."

"You could've at least made an attempt. He's perfect for you. Isn't that right, honey?" Now she's trying to bring Dad into it.

He pretty much ignores everything about my life, too busy raising the perfect minion in Trevor. I'm basically a thorn in their side until I'm married, when they won't give me another thought.

"Nathan seems like a fine young man. His parents wouldn't have raised any less, I'm sure." Great, more fuel for the fire.

"Your dad and I have been discussing our expectations, Lucy, and it's high time you start taking life more seriously and thinking about your future. It would be best if you settled down soon. You're not getting any younger, you know."

Funny that I heard those exact words from someone else recently. Mom hasn't let up since the Whitehalls left tonight, and I'm nearing the end of my rope. I'm so tired of the conversation that what pops out of my mouth next is no fault of my own.

"I'm seeing someone," I announce out of nowhere.

"Well, it can't be that serious if we haven't heard about it until now, which means you're not off the market yet. You should keep in contact with Nathan. I think you two are perfect for each other. Your children would be beautiful," Mom keeps droning on as if I'd said nothing. Beautiful children are all that matter, didn't you know?

What the hell is it going to take? "Actually, it is serious. We're engaged." I internally cringe at the words spewing from my mouth. What the hell am I doing?

Choking on her wine, Mom shrieks, "WHAT? No, you're not. You're not even wearing a ring. You can't be. Franklin, are you hearing this? Your daughter is trying to tell us she's engaged. This is ridiculous." The lie that just came out of my mouth was worth it for no other reason than to see Mom have the biggest fit I've witnessed since I was seven and cut all my hair off.

"I'm hearing it. What I didn't hear is who this man is and why we haven't met him. Care to explain yourself, Lucy?" Well, this is a first—Dad giving a crap about something pertaining to me.

"It's someone I met at the office. We decided not to tell any-one until we had time to—" I'm not able to finish, which is a good thing because I hadn't really come up with an answer yet.

"Oh my God, are you *pregnant*?" my mom asks with a high-pitched shriek.

I really want to fuck with her and say yes, but I'd just be dig-ging myself deeper, and then what? Not only that, but I'm pissed it's what she automatically assumes after telling her I'm engaged.

"No, I'm not pregnant. He's just busy, and we decided not to tell anyone until we could give it the attention it deserves."

Mom's face lights up. "It's Mr. Dubree, isn't it?"

"NO!" I immediately protest.

"Well then, who is it? You said he was from the office." She visibly deflates.

"Mom, Dubree Enterprises is huge." I roll my eyes. "His name is Justin, and he's one of their security officers."

"You're engaged to a rent-a-cop? What are you thinking, Lucy? You're worth more than that," Mom says as she fans herself with her hand dramatically. It doesn't go unnoticed that she didn't say I *deserve* more, but that I'm *worth* more.

And this is precisely what I hate about being home. My par-ents' pretentiousness. It pisses me off. "He's not a rent-a-cop. He runs his own security firm and is a badass bodyguard for the rich and famous." I'm defending my pretend fiancé—this is ridiculous.

Mom sighs in relief. "That sounds slightly more suitable."

I'm so over this conversation.

"You will not marry someone beneath you, and certainly not without our approval," Dad interjects.

"You can't be serious. It's my decision who I marry, and that decision is made." I'm now fighting for my fake engagement.

Seriously, what is wrong with me?

"We'll see about that. Your trust fund says otherwise," Dad states with no emotion whatsoever.

He did not just threaten me.

"Thank you so much for the enlightenment. My trust fund can go fuck itself," I yell my parting words as I walk out of the room, leaving Mom gasping and Dad cursing my name.

3

A NOT SO JOLLY GATHERING

Lucy

"So, then I called my brother to pick me up, who, by the way, was told *not* to come to dinner that night." Lily's jaw drops in shock. She resembled a fish throughout the story about my visit home for Thanksgiving. "There was no way I was spending one more night under their roof. If they're going to hold my trust fund over my head, then they can keep it. I'm doing just fine on my own anyway," I finish.

"Wow, that's harsh. We'll get to the fiancé thing in a minute, but first, why didn't you ever tell me about your family? And more importantly, why *are* you working as a secretary? Does Sebastian know how overqualified you are?"

"I'm not—"

"No. I did not," Sebastian answers from the hallway as he rounds the corner, making my head snap in his direction.

"Why didn't you tell me he was here?" I whisper-shout at Lily. Dammit, I knew I should've left out the part about my parents' harassment over my job. We wanted to catch up after my trip, and I didn't hesitate when she suggested we meet for wine at her place, which also happens to be Sebastian's.

"I figured it wasn't necessary since I'm pretty sure you know his schedule better than I do," Lily says innocently.

At that, Sebastian chuckles—something I rarely see.

"I assumed you'd be out with your brother since she asked me to come here. Sorry," I explain as Sebastian stands next to Lily.

"No need to apologize. You're always welcome. I'm headed out, anyway, so you can enjoy yourselves. Call me when you're done, sweetheart, and I'll come home," he says to Lily before kissing her goodbye. He turns, directing his attention to me. "Don't think I'm dropping this. We'll continue this conversation at the office."

"That won't be necessary," I state.

"I'll be the judge of that," Sebastian responds before walking out the door.

"Thanks a lot," I tell Lily when we're alone.

She snickers. "How did you even land the job? You would think they would have overlooked you for being overqualified, or at least considered you for another position."

"I didn't put my MBA on my resumé. The goal was simplicity, and that's exactly what I got. I'm not looking to complicate my life or become my parents."

"Are you just being stubborn? Because being successful doesn't mean you have to behave like your parents."

I shrug my shoulders. "Maybe. But after this weekend, I'm even more determined to distance myself from them."

"Good luck with that now that you're engaged." Lily laughs.

I groan in frustration. "Oh my God. What am I going to do? They've already called and left two messages. One saying things got slightly out of hand—understatement of the century—and another suggesting I bring him with me at Christmas, that they're *officially extending Justin an invitation for the holiday,*" I say in my snootiest impersonation. "God, could they be any more pretentious? What do you think? Do I tuck my tail between my legs and say we broke it off?"

"Or… I have a better idea. What if you bring him home to meet them?" she asks slyly.

"Yeah, right. Except there isn't anyone to bring." She's looking at me with one raised brow. "What? Should I run an ad for a fake fiancé?" I ask.

"Who says he needs to be fake? I mean, maybe the fiancé part, but the guy doesn't have to be since there really is a Justin, who happens to be a bodyguard *and* has no family to visit for the holidays—which means he could easily play the part."

"Hell no. Not happening. He fricking ghosted me after getting me into bed. I'm never speaking to that jerk again."

"You're obviously still thinking about him since he's the one you just happened to come up with for your fake fiancé," she says pointedly as if she's onto me.

"Only because I'm not good at improvising, and it was easier to use a real person. Otherwise, I don't think about him." *That I'll admit to.*

"If you say so."

"You did it again, Lucy. Another great Christmas party in the books," Eli says, walking up to the bar where I'm sipping my drink.

"I can't take all the credit this time since the hotel's event planner did most of the work. Lily talked me into using her so I could have a good time with everyone else this year."

Usually, I'm so busy with coordination that I don't get to enjoy the party itself, but this is way better. Although, my chattiness is warning me to be careful with how much better it gets.

"Well, I'm glad. It's about time you let loose with the rest of us. Where are Lily and my brother anyway?" he asks as he scans the room.

"You really have to ask?" I laugh. "I'm sure they'll turn up any minute since they've been gone for about ten now," I say, rolling my eyes and making him groan.

"Damn, those two are obnoxious." He shakes his head with a smirk on his face.

"Eh, they're cute. It's hard to find that kind of connection, let alone with someone you want to spend the rest of your life with. I'm happy for them."

"Yeah, you're right. Maybe I'm just jealous."

"Tell me about it."

After that, we fall into an easy silence, sipping our drinks at the bar as we people watch.

"Let's go get our seats for dinner. I think they're starting the salads, and I'm starving." Lily breaks our silence abruptly as she bounds up to us with Sebastian on her heels.

"I bet since you probably just worked up an appetite," Eli teases her as Sebastian smirks.

"Oh, hush, it's your brother's fault. Now, come on, let's eat," Lily says, pulling me toward the tables.

As we round the corner to the banquet hall, I halt and do a double take. "Wait. What's he doing here?" I ask apprehensively.

Lily looks up. "Who?"

"Justin!" I whisper, knowing Sebastian and Eli aren't far behind.

She leans in. "Oh, yeah. Sebastian wanted extra security for the event tonight. He still freaks out at things like this, 'cause… well, you know," she responds quietly before straightening and turning to the guys. "Sebastian, I'd love another glass of champagne. It might be faster if you get it at the bar. Would you mind? Lucy, do you want Eli to grab you something?" she asks without missing a beat.

"Uh, sure. I'll take champagne as well." I know exactly what she's doing. If I were smart, I would have said no to avoid this conversation.

As I knew she would, Lily starts in when we reach our table. "Lucy, he's right there. It's the perfect opportunity to start a conversation and see if he has plans for Christmas."

"No, Lily, I mean it. I'm sure he wants nothing to do with me, and I certainly don't want anything to do with him." I shudder.

"Then what's your plan? Have you told your parents the engagement's off?"

"I figured I'd wait until I'm there, so they don't have time to set me up with anyone else."

She nods in agreement. "And you're sure your brother won't rat you out?"

"He would never. He understands. Hell, he'd probably find a stand-in for me if I wanted him to." I roll my eyes. "That's too complicated, though. And what's the point, since it won't matter after Christmas when I'll tell them we broke up anyway."

"Just think how easy it would be, though, if you had Justin with you and didn't have to worry about it. You know you have chemistry already. It would be perfect."

"Well, apparently, it was one-sided. Can we drop it now?"

Luckily, she has no choice when Eli and Sebastian return with our drinks.

My thoughts stay on Justin the rest of the meal as I steal glances his way while he walks the perimeter of the room, keeping an eye out for anything suspicious. At one point, I think I see him looking in my direction from my peripheral vision, but I can't tell for sure. By the time my eyes reach him, his head is turned away. What I can tell is that I'd forgotten how damn sexy he is. Now that I've started checking him out, I can't seem to stop.

My mind keeps imagining what would happen if he did come home as my fake fiancé. Would we rekindle our connection? Regardless of how his dismissal felt, I'm sure there was something between us. How did he walk away so easily? My biggest fear is that it somehow relates to my bedroom skills, which probably has something to do with why I haven't been close to anyone since then.

Asking him could give me answers or put these stupid thoughts to rest once and for all. But then again, it's ridiculous to consider since there's no way he would do it. Not to mention, Christmas is only three weeks away; I'm sure he has plans already. But what if he doesn't?

Ugh. It doesn't matter because I can't risk asking only to be humiliated again. It's not worth another blow to my ego. A girl can only handle so much rejection. That he hasn't even acknowledged my presence tonight should be proof enough that he isn't interested.

I'm distracted from my spiraling thoughts when Jordan asks me to dance after dinner is over and the band starts playing. Lily gives me a wink before I go. She was right about him being cute. He's also sweet, saying Lily had mentioned me and that he would have already asked me out, but that he's been busy and hadn't found the time yet.

Halfway through the song, I've decided I wouldn't be opposed to going on a date with him and am even excited by the prospect, until something catches my eye at the edge of the dance floor—or rather, someone… who finally decides to make some very aggressive eye contact.

"Are you okay?" Jordan asks, alerting me to the fact that I've stopped moving.

"Oh my gosh, yeah. Sorry, I just realized I need to go to the bathroom." *Wow, Lucy, way to go.*

"Oh, okay. I'll catch up with you later then," he says, probably thinking I'm crazy.

"Definitely, and sorry, it just sort of hit me." *Oh my God, kill me now.*

I walk away in a hurry, anxious to leave my mortification behind. Stopping at the table to grab my purse, it doesn't take long for Lily to catch up and enter the bathroom right behind me.

"Lucy, what are you doing? I saw you practically run from the dance floor. Did he say something to upset you?"

"No, Jordan was super nice. And you were right about him being good-looking."

"Then what the heck? You look like you saw a ghost."

I drop my head into my hands, groaning before lifting it back up. "Justin finally looked at me. Like, really *looked* at me. He was right there, Lily, just staring from the sideline, and I froze. Oh my God, I feel like such an idiot." Telling her about my swift departure sounds as bad as I remember it, making her laugh. At least one of us is.

"You're not an idiot, but I don't think you're over Justin."

"There's nothing to get over. He ghosted me as if I were nothing to him. And now I've probably ruined my chances with Jordan because of the jerk."

"Do you think maybe he did it on purpose? He avoided you all night, and then when you dance with another guy, he makes sure you see him. Maybe there's more there than you think."

"Whether it was intentional or not doesn't matter—the door is closed. You know, I just realized how tired I am. I think I'm just gonna head home. Let's go back to the table so I can say goodbye."

"Fine. But I bet Jordan will still ask you out. I saw you two out there, and he seemed really into you," she says as we walk out.

"Yeah, we'll see about that."

Upon hearing of my departure, Sebastian insists on having the company car drive me home, and he doesn't get any protest from me until he waves Tom over to escort me out. Unsurprisingly, I don't win the argument, and the next thing I know, Tom's leading me toward the exit.

Awkward, since the last time we were together, we were playing tonsil hockey. I'm hoping he's not expecting a repeat when his hand finds my lower back as we walk. However, it doesn't look like he'll get the opportunity because before we make it out of the banquet hall, someone else's hand lands on his shoulder.

"I'll take her from here, Tom. Go ahead and take my post while I'm gone," Justin tells him.

Tom turns his head but doesn't remove his hand. "It's okay. I'll make sure she gets to the car safely."

"It wasn't a request," Justin states with a pointed look that says *don't fuck with me.*

This is ridiculous. "I'm fine walking out on my own," I interject.

"That's not an option," Justin states.

"Then I'd prefer Tom take me," I respond, lifting my chin slightly.

"Your preference wasn't asked for. Let's go." He grabs my arm and propels me forward, leaving a bewildered Tom behind.

"What do you think you're doing?" I wrench my arm from his grasp.

"What does it look like? I'm seeing you out."

Storming ahead of him until I reach the doors to leave, I suddenly stop to face the man who, until twenty minutes ago, hadn't given me the time of day and wouldn't even look at me.

"I don't need you to make sure I'm safe. In fact, you're the last man who should have that responsibility since your respect and concern for me rank in the negatives." Turning abruptly, I shove the door open and rush to the car, flinging myself inside to escape.

The door doesn't shut quickly enough to avoid hearing Justin's booming voice as he calls out, "Lucy, wait!"

But I don't.

4

ALL I WANT FOR CHRISTMAS

Lucy

THE NEXT DAY, I SIT ON LILY'S COUCH WHILE SHE PATIENTLY listens to my pity party. I don't know what I'd do without her at this point. She's been such a good sport, hearing me drone on for the last hour now.

"That's two men who are now out of the question because of one man who has absolutely no right to interfere," I say before taking another big gulp of wine.

"To be fair, you didn't even want one of them."

"That's not the point," I argue.

"But it's true."

"The point is, Justin made it clear he wanted nothing to do with me. The man's had six months to change his mind or at least explain himself. It's too late now. He's like a bad dream I can't wake up from."

"You know this is a sign, right? You're going home in three weeks—why don't you ask him to go with you? He owes it to you at this point. Plus, he was obviously trying to talk to you last night, so the door is wide open, in my opinion." She reaches out to clink her glass with mine. "Cheers. You're welcome."

I lift my glass to my mouth and take a drink instead. "I am not cheersing to that. I'm sticking with my plan to tell them we broke up on the flight over. I'll keep up the charade until then to avoid another date with Nathan while I'm there. It's perfect."

"They'll be able to sneak a dinner in by the time you leave if they find out you're single again on day one. It would be so much easier if you had a legit reason not to be set up with someone."

"Ugh, I know it would, trust me. But seriously, it's not an option. I'm not going to play the damsel in distress to get his attention, especially since I don't even want it."

In the Uber—an hour and two more glasses of wine later—my mind has other ideas because my fingers betray my common sense and type out a message to Justin that will surely get a response with a bit of manipulation. Knowing Justin's protective nature, getting his attention isn't rocket science.

Justin

It crossed my mind initially when I agreed to work the Christmas party for Mr. Dubree that I'd undoubtedly see Lucy there, but at the time, my momentary lapse in judgment told me it was no big deal. In hindsight, it was a very big deal. She's been a distraction from the day I walked into Sebastian Dubree's office to the day I failed Lily, and now still—six months later.

I blamed that distraction for letting Lily slip through the cracks.

Ending things with Lucy was my solution and, likely, my self-imposed punishment. Regardless of whether it was the right thing to do, the way I went about it was wrong. Knowing I wouldn't be strong enough to do it in person or otherwise, I simply tried pretending she didn't exist. It definitely didn't work.

My wandering eyes couldn't refrain from stealing a glance in her direction every few minutes last night. She was just as beautiful as I remembered, even more so with that sexy red holiday dress sparkling against her porcelain skin. Her long, luscious blonde hair hanging down her back reminded me of our last morning together. It had fanned over my face as she rode me that final time before breakfast, right before I walked out the door of the most amazing night I'd ever had.

My body moved closer of its own accord when I saw her dancing with that other man. Remembering the feel of my hands on her hips made me wish it were me holding her close while our bodies swayed to the music. I'd done so well maintaining distance and keeping my gaze from meeting hers until I could no longer stop myself from intentionally catching her eye.

As she scrambled to the ladies' room, I knew she was affected, and if Lily hadn't followed, I would have gone after her. Then, when Tom put his hand on her, the remaining threads of my willpower snapped, and I was incapable of stopping my interference. Again, she became a defenseless distraction, one I decided then and there to stop fighting.

I didn't speak the truth that struggled to break free soon enough: how sorry I was for my behavior, how much our time together truly meant to me, and how much I've missed her ever since. Before I worked up the nerve, she laid into me about not respecting her, which she had every right to do. Hearing the anger in her final words and watching her run away, ignoring my plea to wait, only confirmed what I'd already suspected—that I was too late.

Until this afternoon when my phone lit up with the name I never expected to see…

> Lucy: I've gotten myself into some trouble. Would you be willing to meet? You're the only one I can think of who could help.

It must be serious if she's resorted to asking for my help. After she took off, I didn't think I'd ever hear from her again. And why now? Did something happen today, or did my presence last night make her think of me for something she was already dealing with? I won't disappoint her again, so there's only one way to respond.

> Me: Tell me when and where, and I'll be there.
>
> Lucy: Can you come over now? To my place?
>
> Me: See you in twenty.

My mind spins over what could be wrong during the drive. Of the five dates we went on, there were no red flags, no reason to suspect she was into anything shady. Her job was normal. Her condo wasn't out of the ordinary for a woman her age with her salary. She didn't overindulge any evening we were together, nor was she under the influence of anything.

I'm at a complete loss as I knock on her door seconds before it swings open abruptly.

"Hi. You came," she says with a look of bewilderment.

"I said I'd see you in twenty minutes." My eyebrows slant in confusion.

"Based on the last time you said you'd see me, I wasn't sure," she responds flippantly.

I catch a slight slur in her speech. "I deserve that. Have you been drinking?"

"Maybe." She shrugs. "You know what? This is a bad idea. Never mind." She starts to close the door.

My hand stops it. "Lucy, what's going on? I'm not leaving until I get some answers."

She whips the door wide open. "Oh really? You're going to demand answers? What about when I needed answers? Like why you ghosted me. Or why, instead of acting like an adult, you decided to ignore me and never speak to me again. Did I get answers? No. So if you expect me to just—"

Barging forward, I sling her over my shoulder and slam the door shut while she shouts in protest, pounding on my back. Stomping to the living room, I gently place her on the couch.

"What in God's name is going on, Lucy? I'm not leaving until you tell me what trouble you're in so I can help." My arms are crossed as I stand before her, giving her no room to get up.

"How dare you? You can't just barge in here and act like a beast. You have no right after the way you left things."

"Your text a little while ago says otherwise. You're the one who brought me here, so get on with it. This can go the easy way or the hard way—you choose." I'm nearing my breaking point, and if she doesn't start explaining what this is about, there's no telling what I'll do next.

"What's that supposed to mean?" she asks, the slightest trepidation in her voice.

Fuck. My goal isn't to scare her more, but dammit… If she needs help, then I need to know with what. This is not how I expected things to go on the drive over. Maybe it's time for a different tactic.

Taking a seat on the couch, I turn toward her, resting my arm on the back of the cushion, concentrating on softening my tone. "Listen, Lucy, we have a past that, unfortunately, didn't end as it should have. But I'm here now, and I'd like to help in whatever way possible. Please let me do what I can to make up for the way I've treated you."

My words have the desired effect, and she relaxes immediately. Thank God. I'm not sure what the problem is, but something is obviously wrong if she's drinking and texting me out of the blue on a Sunday afternoon, especially after the way she left last night.

"All right, but you'll probably say no. It's crazy that I'm even suggesting it." She brings her feet up to the couch, bending her knees and hugging them to her body.

"Let me be the judge of that. What do you need?" I'm trying hard to keep my patience in check as she battles with herself to answer.

"A fiancé," she blurts as she looks up at the ceiling, blowing air from her lungs.

What the…? I'm speechless and unable to form words for a moment.

"Yeah, so see? It's not something you can help me with anyway. I'm sorry. The wine went to my head this afternoon, and I just… God, this is so stupid." She rolls her eyes and then drops her head between her knees, shaking it back and forth while groaning.

After another minute of silent perplexity, I gently pry her head up and turn her to face me before finally finding my voice again. "What do you mean you need a fiancé?"

I watch as she contemplates her words, probably deciding whether to elaborate or keep up her efforts to blow it off, which won't work if she chooses that route. The moment her mind is made up, she sighs in indignation.

"My family's complicated—so complicated that I only go home to visit twice a year, on Thanksgiving and Christmas. A few weeks ago, at Thanksgiving, they were putting pressure on me to go out with this guy and then said it was time for me to settle down and start taking life seriously. To them, that means getting married to someone they approve of, becoming the perfect wife, and having perfect babies. They were ready to plan more dates during my visit for Christmas, but I panicked and told them I was engaged." She looks at me sheepishly before quickly continuing. I'm trying to take it all in, wondering why she called *me* for this.

"At first, I just told them I was already involved with someone, but they were relentless, insisting I should give this Nathan guy a chance. So, in the heat of the moment, I went a step further and said we were engaged. It turned into a huge argument, and I ended up walking out. A few days later, they apologized and said we would discuss it more while I'm home for Christmas." She's cringing as she finishes.

"When you say 'we,' who did you tell them you were engaged to?" This is nowhere near any of the scenarios that went through my mind on my way here. Where the hell is she going with this? I have an idea, but...

"Since I'm a terrible liar, I named the only person who came to mind, someone I knew enough about to be able to bullshit my way through..." She pauses and takes a deep breath before finishing, "so, I told them I was engaged to you." She looks up shyly.

This is the moment I know I'll do anything she asks and be anyone she needs—whatever it takes to get more time with her looking at me with those piercing baby blues, even though it's the last thing I deserve.

Before any words leave my mouth, she goes on, "But actually, it's all good. I've already decided to tell them we broke up as soon as I get there, and then it won't matter. Really, I think the—"

"What do you need me to do?" I cut her off. Hearing her breakup plan affects me more than it should, and I need to know if she was about to ask what I'm hoping for.

"Well, I thought… maybe you could pretend to be my fiancé and come home with me for Christmas, but I'm sure—"

"I'll do it." *Thank fuck.*

"Wait. Are you serious? You'd be gone a whole week, and you'd be spending Christmas without your family. Not only that, but you'd have to act as if you like me. Actually, you'd need to make it look like you love me."

"I usually spend the holidays with my buddies, but they have each other, so I'm good there. As far as faking an engagement and pretending to be in love? I don't know." I shrug. "Sounds like a fun holiday to me."

"You say that now, but you might be singing a different tune after you meet my parents."

"Ah, they can't be that bad if they raised you."

"Says the guy who ding-dong ditched me."

"Aaand that's my cue to go." I stand up and look down at her. "Send me your flight information so I can book mine. The sooner, the better. I need to make arrangements at the office for my absence, and let me know if I need to pack anything special." I get up and start heading toward the front door.

"I'll take care of your flight. It's the least I can do since this is such a big ask."

I turn with my hand on the doorknob. "Not happening. I'll book my own flight. Send me the details if you want me to go. See you later, Lucy."

"Justin—"

But I'm already stepping out and shutting the door before she can argue.

5

ONE GOLDEN RING

Lucy

"S ERIOUSLY, THANKS FOR DOING THIS." I'M STILL IN DISBELIEF, and we're mere hours from my hometown.

After Justin left the day of my tipsy texting, my mind came out of its wine fog and realized too late what I'd done. Once he agreed to go home with me, he left abruptly, infuriatingly insisting on booking his own flight. Not only that, but he bumped me to first class so we could sit together.

While it might have been necessary since I needed to give him the lowdown on my family, I'm not sure how he'll feel about paying for it when he finds out how wealthy my family is. I still haven't told him about that, only that they have certain standards that are hard to live up to.

With two connecting flights, I took the easy route and told

him all about my brother, who promised he'd be at the airport to pick me up this time. Since Trevor knows the truth, I figured it'd be an easier start to the week and assumed Justin would be relieved someone knew about our phony relationship, but he actually seemed put off by it, which was weird.

"If you thank me again, I'm taking the next flight home instead of making our connection. Now, tell me the rest of what I need to know to make this believable," he says, taking a bite of his taco.

We're sitting in a Mexican restaurant in the airport during our two-hour layover. The tacos are good, but the margaritas are better, and liquid courage is exactly what I need for this. I'm still not sure how we're going to pull this off when I secretly want to rip his heart out like he did mine. Instead, I'm supposed to act like I'm in love with the guy.

I stick to the basics while we eat, only giving him names, jobs, and a few hobbies before calling it good. It's not like any couple talks nonstop about their family, so too much information would be overdoing it. He'll know all he needs to soon enough.

"Why do you only go home twice a year?" he asks, catching me off guard. I'd forgotten that slipped out during my explanation for this mess. Throughout our previous dates all those months ago, I happily avoided talking about my family. Instead, most of our conversations were centered on our likes and dislikes, favorite shows, hobbies, places we'd like to visit… those sorts of things.

"I'm busy with work, and I have a life. I can't get away all the time." That's reasonable.

"What drew you to San Diego in the first place? Seems far from home. Did you go to school there?" He's asking way too many questions. Freaking him out about what he'll be walking into is probably not the best idea at this point. I need to shut this down somehow.

"I wanted to experience a different part of the country. The West Coast intrigued me. It's an entirely different ocean, different climate, and new people. What about you? Did you grow up in San Diego?"

"No. The military brought me there, and I ended up staying. So, explain why you didn't just tell your parents 'no' to dating some rando instead of lying about being engaged." Justin quickly veers the conversation back to me. We're halfway through the meal and two drinks in.

I shrug and down my second margarita, signaling the waitress for another. I'll take all the help I can get.

"That's it? No comment?" he asks, taking a bite of his taco while he waits for an answer.

"It was just a heat of the moment thing. They were relentless, and I didn't like how they disregarded my relationship." I'm still sore over it.

"Your *fake* relationship." He smirks.

"Hey, they didn't know that. What if you and I *had* been dating, and my parents tried to set me up with this guy? Then how would you feel?" I reply smugly.

"First of all, if you and I were really dating, you bet your ass I'd have known your parents by then, and I sure as hell wouldn't have given them a chance to set you up with someone else. Not on my watch."

With the alcohol setting in and a fresh drink in hand, I'm feeling more mouthy than usual. "Oh really, if we'd been dating, huh? That's funny, coming from the guy who ran at the first sign of an actual relationship. Oh, I know… maybe you could give Nathan a few tips on how to get me into his bed while you're there. I'm sure my parents would appreciate it."

"Lucy, that's enough."

But I continue my rant, the alcohol taking control, "Speaking of enough, maybe you should be giving me a few tips since I'm obviously not enough when it comes to sex. I mean, why else would you never call me again? Unless you only wanted to see how long it would take for me to fuck you." I lift my drink to take a sip, but before I reach my mouth, Justin leans forward and wraps his hand around mine, slowly lowering my glass back to the table.

"Let's get a few things straight. Most importantly, your skills in the bedroom are not an issue. I'm pretty sure the four orgasms I had that night prove it. As for adding a notch to my bedpost, I don't waste time on dates for those. I don't need to. And just to clarify, the two extra dates before we *fucked*? That was because I knew the more the anticipation grew, the better it would be. And baby? It was explosive." He lifts his hand from mine and sits back like he didn't just light my core on fire. And did he just quote my final text from months ago?

I have no idea how to respond, so I take another sip of my drink in avoidance. This is going to be the longest week of my life.

Justin

Damn this woman is feisty. Not that she doesn't have every right to be, but fuck is it going to be hard to manage myself around her. All I want to do is remind her exactly how explosive we are. The memory of it makes my dick swell underneath the table. At least she's quiet for a moment, giving me a minute to cool my jets and get my thoughts under control.

She needs to vent, and it's less than I deserve. I should've let her have her moment, but there was no way I was about to leave her thinking she was the problem. What kills me is that she's probably been thinking these things ever since then. I'm an asshole for not explaining. It's not Lucy's fault I'm too weak when it comes to her, but she's suffering because of it.

Hopefully, I've put some of her worries to rest. I'm going to have to get myself in check if I'm hoping to survive this week without losing my head again. Seeing her flushed cheeks from my speech tells me I'm not the only one with a problem. We need a safer topic.

"So, tell me about your family's Christmas traditions."

"Hmm… okay. On Christmas Eve, we each open one present, which is always a pair of pajamas. Then we put out milk and cookies for Santa and carrots for the reindeer. I try staying up every year to catch him, but I swear my parents put sleeping pills in my drink at night because I always fall asleep and miss seeing him."

She looks so sincere that I can't tell if she's kidding, and I'm not sure what to say—until she bursts out laughing, and I deflate with relief.

"Oh my God, the look on your face was priceless. You seriously thought I still believed in Santa? Wow, you really do think I'm crazy," she says, causing me to laugh along with her.

"Crazy or not, with acting skills like that, I'm definitely not worried about our performance this week." Holding my glass up, she meets me halfway to clink our glasses together.

"We better finish these up and get to our gate. We're boarding in ten," I say, signing the check.

"I'm on it," Lucy assures me, knocking back her drink.

Lucy passes out minutes after we board the next flight and is currently drooling in my lap. I'm sure her nerves are going haywire at having to pull this off. I know mine are. Having to convince her parents that we're engaged when Lucy would prefer to push me off a cliff might be somewhat of a challenge.

Don't get me wrong, I'm on cloud nine to be spending the week with the woman who worked her way into my heart so quickly. I haven't stopped thinking about her since that horrible day all those months ago, and I've regretted every minute without her. She doesn't realize she's handed me a second chance, and it's up to me to make the most of this week and rectify my mistakes. While I'm not sure how to do that yet, I'm determined to figure it out.

My mind swirls with what she's told me about her family so far, which isn't a whole lot. She's been pretty elusive about her relationship with her parents. I'm anxious to meet them to satisfy my growing curiosity about why she resorted to telling them such a huge lie when she could have just said no. It confounds me how she can be so strong and capable in her personal life while still cowering to her parents.

I'm not happy with her brother knowing the truth about us. It would be easier if everyone were on the same page. This only makes it uncomfortable having to blatantly pretend to be something we're not in the face of someone who knows it's all bullshit. It complicates the situation rather than putting me at ease, which I could tell was what she was going for.

Another issue is that Lucy seems to have forgotten how to be comfortable around me, which won't bode well when she introduces me to her parents. So, as much as I'd like to let her sleep since I'm enjoying her nestled up against me, it's time for some practice during the last hour of our flight, and I've been looking forward to this all day.

My hand slowly rubs her back as I brush her hair from her face. "Lucy, it's time to wake up, baby."

Her eyes blink open slowly as she asks, "We're landing?"

I chuckle softly. "No, we have about an hour left, but we need to deal with a few more things before we get there. Here, I got you some water while you were out." She grabs it as she rises from my chest.

"Thanks. Sorry, I didn't mean to crash on you. Man, those margaritas hit me hard."

I scoff as she guzzles it down. "Yeah, you can say that again. Three will do that to someone your size who doesn't usually drink that much."

"Apparently. Anyway, what else do we need to go over? I think I covered enough to make it through the week."

"You did… but there's a couple things you forgot about, baby."

"What's with the baby? And I think I'd know if I forgot something about my own family, so enlighten me, oh wise one."

"Well, for starters, you realize you'll have to treat me a little differently in front of your parents—as in nicer?" She rolls her eyes until I reach for her hand, causing her to look down and furrow her brows. "And you'll have to get used to me touching you. I'm a very affectionate fiancé." I run my thumb along her cheekbone, cupping her chin while caressing her hand. "Can you handle it?"

Her eyes widen as I slowly lean in for a kiss when she pulls back hastily, snapping her hand back. "What are you doing? You can't kiss me!"

"Will that be your reaction in front of your parents?" I smirk.

"You're not going to kiss me in front of them."

"Oh? So they'll never see your fiancé show you affection?" She doesn't answer quickly enough, so I continue, "Should we try that again?" I raise my eyebrows in question.

"Uhhh… I hadn't thought that far ahead. I mean, I don't know. I don't think PDA is proper in front of parentals, so… no?"

"Think again, Lucy. If we're going to make them believe we're so in love that we're engaged, we'll have to be convincing. You don't want them to see through it and keep trying to set you up over the next year, do you?" I've got her right where I want her.

"No."

"That's what I thought." My head dips as my hand wraps around her neck and pulls her in.

The moment our lips touch, I'm in heaven. This is where I belong. She feels like home, and I've finally returned after a long journey. Too long. It's been way… too… fucking long since I've had my lips on hers.

Within seconds, neither of us can hold back our moans as the kiss progresses. When her mouth parts, my tongue sneaks in to find its mate, reveling in the feel of her softness, seeking more. Her hands grab my head fiercely, deepening the kiss. This is what I remember. Our chemistry is off the charts.

Unfortunately, if I don't stop now, we'll be joining the mile-high club, and there's one more critical piece to our deception that needs to be taken care of. So, I reluctantly pull back to a dazed Lucy, causing my balls to tighten. Fuck, what I wouldn't give to keep going right now.

"You have no idea how difficult that was to stop, baby."

"Why did you then?" she asks impishly, retreating into her seat, making me chuckle.

"Because we're running out of time, and there's an essential part of this you didn't think about."

"What now?" *So sassy.*

"We're engaged, right?"

She nods.

"What's the first thing people usually ask to see when you tell them you're engaged?"

Understanding dawns. "Oh shit. I don't have a ring. I can't believe I didn't think of that. Mom even asked me about it the minute she heard, and I came up with some bullshit reason. Crap." She slaps her forehead with the palm of her hand.

"It's a good thing you have such a smart fiancé then," I say as I reach into the breast pocket of my shirt.

Her hand flies to her mouth when she registers what I'm doing. "What…? How did you…?" I notice the second the light bulb comes on in her head. "Wait a minute—is that why Lily randomly asked me to go ring shopping with her last week 'for fun'?" She makes air quotes. "Why didn't you just tell me?"

"Because this is so much better." I smile and reach for her hand. "Would you like me to do the honors?" I present the two-carat princess-cut solitaire encased in thick gold prongs with diamonds between each one. I slowly slide it onto her finger while her eyes widen in shock.

"Holy shit! Why did you get such a big one? Please tell me it's borrowed. It didn't need to be real; we could've just used a knockoff." Her hand is shaking as I slide it on.

"I'm not letting my fiancé, fake or not, walk around in a cubic zirconia knockoff or anything less than she deserves. Plus, do you want your parents to question the stability of your future husband if they look too closely?" Once the ring is in place, I bring her hand to my lips and kiss it.

The flight attendant announces we're making our final descent, and I look at Lucy, wondering if she'll ever take her eyes off the ring.

"I'd say we're all set. Though we should practice showing our affection some more." I wiggle my eyebrows. That gets her attention.

"Ha. Nice try, buddy."

6

JOY TO THE WEALTH

Lucy

USING THE EXCUSE OF NEEDING TO FRESHEN UP, WE STOP at the first bathroom we see after deboarding the plane. Once I'm hidden in a stall, it takes me seconds to sink down and hold my hand out in front of me. *Holy shit.* This ring is humongous… and beautiful… and not mine. I'm practically hyperventilating from the emotions rising to the surface at having it on my finger.

What was I thinking when I asked Justin to do this, and what the hell was he thinking when he agreed? At least I have wine to blame. Justin has nothing. This can't really be happening, can it? I'm about to introduce Justin to my brother. At least he knows what's going on. I'm starting to regret not giving my parents a heads-up that he's with me. Even though they did extend the invitation, I didn't want to answer a million questions beforehand. Oh well, too late now.

I'm not sure how this is going to play out. He thinks I gave him enough information, but it wasn't nearly enough to prepare him for what he's about to walk into. My parents are going to rip him to shreds. I'm pretty sure Justin isn't used to this level of wealth. Although, you'd think otherwise with the size of this ring. I still can't wrap my head around it.

Realizing I'm taking too long, I hurry to freshen up before walking out.

"I was about to send the cavalry in for you," Justin says as soon as I join him.

"Sorry, I just needed a minute before we see Trevor," I explain.

"I take it you're nervous?" His eyebrows raise in question.

"Yeah, I guess I am. I shouldn't be since he knows, but it's weird having him meet you, period." I look at Justin sheepishly, seeing the understanding in his eyes.

"The good news is that if this were a real introduction to your fiancé, you'd be nervous, so you're fine. I'm sure it's no different meeting a girlfriend's family for the first time, so I think I'm in the clear being nervous myself."

"What do you mean you're sure it isn't? Have you never met any of your girlfriend's families?"

"I'm not one for girlfriends."

"Yeah. That makes sense. Sure wish I would've known that before you walked out on me." I'm shaking my head as I start walking toward baggage claim.

"Lucy, that's not what happened," he pleads, grabbing for my arm, but I pull away before he does.

"It's exactly what happened, but you know what? Save it for someone who cares," I say, turning and heading toward the exit.

He sighs loudly as he trudges alongside me, and I can see him shaking his head in exasperation. Too bad. He made his bed, and now he can sleep in it.

When I enter the arrivals area, my brother and I immediately make eye contact while Justin trails behind. Thank God Trevor didn't let me down. He's exactly what I need to get me through these next few hours.

"Hey, Luce," he says, wrapping me in a hug.

"Thanks for coming. I'm so glad you're here… seriously," I say into his shoulder, not ready for the inevitable.

"I told you I would be. You don't have to act like it's a miracle or anything." He laughs as he pulls away.

"Right now, it feels like it. I can't believe I'm doing this. By the way—Trevor, this is Justin. Justin, this is my brother, Trevor." I motion to each of them as I make introductions.

Justin sticks his hand out toward Trevor. "Hey, man, it's good to meet you. Your sister's told me a lot about you. She speaks highly of you."

Trevor shakes his hand with indignation. "Yeah, wish I could say the same, but no can do. Hopefully, you won't disappear on us this week. From what I hear, you don't seem to have a great track record with that."

Oh shit.

Justin looks at me pointedly. I guess the cat's out of the bag that not only does Trevor know we're not engaged, but that Justin is on my shit list. Which means he's also on Trevor's shit list.

"Right. Why don't we go get our bags before they think we

abandoned them? Come on." I hook my arm through Trevor's and drag him toward baggage claim.

"You didn't have to start things out that way," I whisper low enough for only him to hear.

"I'm not going to be friendly with the guy who broke my sister's heart. You can't expect me to be nice to the douchebag."

"You'll have to be in front of Mom and Dad. If not, they'll wonder what your problem is and dig for an answer. They'll already be looking for any red flags as it is. Don't screw this up for me. And he didn't break my heart, asshole. He just ghosted me, no big deal." I try to play it off.

"Lucy, you're an open book. I could hear the hurt in your voice when you told me the story. You're a terrible liar." He's looking at me pointedly when his eyes veer downward and widen.

"Holy shit! Check out that rock. How the hell did I miss that thing?" Trevor pauses mere steps from the baggage carousel and grabs my hand, inspecting the thing like he's a diamond expert or something. "Well shit, I figured it'd be a fake, but this is definitely the real McCoy. What did you do, borrow it from a friend?"

Justin stands to the side, arms crossed, while Trevor makes a spectacle about the ring. It doesn't look like he's going to help me out with this. Yep, he's for sure not.

"I'll go grab the bags," he says, stalking off.

"No, I didn't borrow it. Justin gave it to me before we got off the plane. It's just for the week. I'm giving it back—obviously."

"Dude, what did you say this guy does again? This is worth some bucks. Looks like you might just be able to pull this off, little sis." He drops my hand as Justin joins us with our bags.

"Gee, thanks," I say to my brother, rolling my eyes.

"Way to go on the ring, man. You may be a prick, but you

have good taste in jewelry. That'll be a good start with the parents," Trevor says to a scowling Justin.

"You might want to lighten up on the jabs. I'd hate for you to slip up in front of an audience," Justin responds.

"Nah, it'll be fine. It's normal for a big brother to be protective of his little sister. I wouldn't blow your cover anyway… for Lucy's sake. But if you fuck with her while you're under my roof, then be prepared," Trevor threatens.

"Trevor, he's a bodyguard. I'm pretty sure he'd win in a fight. But thanks for the chivalry." I lean up and kiss him on the cheek.

"I know people," Trevor deadpans.

"Trevor, knock it off." I smack his arm. "Can we go already?"

Justin, however, decides to get the last word in.

"If I hurt your sister again, you have free rein to kick my ass. But I can't guarantee there'll be no fucking… with her while I'm here," Justin quips.

"Oh my God. I'm leaving now. Follow me or not—I don't care at this point." Without waiting for an answer, I turn on my heels and stalk toward the exit.

All I can think as we make our way to the car is not only will this be the longest week of my life, but at this rate, it's shaping up to be the week from hell.

"Nice ride. What is it you do again?" Justin asks, perplexed, as the lights flash on my brother's Maserati.

"Fuck off mostly," Trevor answers, earning another slap to his arm.

"Shut up, Trevor. That's not true. I know for a fact you're one of the top agents in the office. I'm still in touch with people on the inside, you know," I counter his statement.

"Aw, are you checking up on me, little sis?" he teases as he pops the trunk, each man loading a bag.

"No, but your name sure comes up a lot when I'm talking to Suzie," I taunt.

"Christ, I can't believe you're still friends with that gold digger. She won't leave me alone. You need to be more selective of those you surround yourself with." He pointedly looks in Justin's direction.

"God, you're such a brat," I say as I open the door to the back seat. I'm about to get in when Justin steps beside me.

"Hey, sit up front with your brother. I'll take the back," he says.

"No way, you're too big to fit back here. I'm fine. Or are you scared to be that close to him?" I laugh and hop in, hearing him grumble as he shuts the door.

Justin

Just great. I knew Lucy and her brother were close, but I never imagined they were close enough for her to divulge our short-lived relationship and how it ended. That could put a crimp in my plan to woo her back. My instincts tell me Trevor won't hesitate to regularly remind Lucy why she shouldn't give me another chance.

I'll have to play it cool around him and keep my efforts behind closed doors. It would benefit me to win him over, but whether that's possible is a big question and not my priority this week. Winning Lucy back is.

Luckily, they continue their banter during the drive, giving me plenty of time to mentally prepare for what's next. I'm doing this for Lucy, and I want to make it as easy as possible for her, which means earning her parents' approval. So, I spend most of the drive going over possible questions they might ask and considering my answers.

I take in our surroundings as we exit the freeway. It's a clean area with high-end commercial spaces, and based on the general feel, I'd say it's a pretty bougie part of town. We take a few more turns before driving along the coast, where multimillion-dollar houses sprawl between us and the ocean. We turn off, coming to a gate, and a guard waves us through.

A minute later, we pull up to another gate at the entrance to a driveway, where Trevor rolls down the window and enters a code before it swings open. As we go around a curve, the house—or rather, the mansion—in front of me says all I need to know.

"Welcome to the Alcott Family Estate, where the wealthy want for nothing," Trevor says as he pulls around the enormous fountain in the middle of the driveway and parks his car in front of a set of stairs leading up to a massive front porch with four three-foot-wide marble pillars supporting the veranda above.

Wealthy is an understatement.

"This is where you grew up?" I ask in awe of the grandeur, to either one willing to answer. As I speak, a man opens the back door for Lucy.

"All eighteen years," she answers before climbing out, greeting the man as Darryl.

Exiting simultaneously, I join Lucy as she turns to introduce me. "This is my fiancé, Justin Burns. Justin, this is our house manager, Darryl." She looks embarrassed as she makes the introduction, and I'm not sure if it's because of me or the fact that they have a house manager.

"Congratulations, Miss Lucy. It's a pleasure to welcome you,

Mr. Burns. I've been serving the Alcotts for twenty years now. Don't hesitate to let me know if you need anything to make your stay more comfortable." He shakes my hand and bows slightly. What the hell have I gotten myself into?

"Please, call me Justin. It's nice to meet you, Darryl. I'm sure I'll be fine but thank you." I walk to the back of the car for the bags, only to have Darryl rush over to stop me.

"No, you head on in, and I'll take care of the bags. That's my job, sir."

"Okay, thank you, Darryl," I return.

Lucy and Trevor stand by, waiting. Trevor looks amused, clearly recognizing the bewilderment on my face, while Lucy appears uneasy, making me want to sling her over my shoulder and leave this all behind. Instead, I drape my arm over her shoulder and give her a playful squeeze.

"You ready to introduce me to my future in-laws?" I lean down and kiss her forehead as she looks at me like a deer in headlights, Trevor chuckling in the background. "It's okay, baby. We've got this," I whisper in her ear and nuzzle her for a second while I'm there, breathing in her scent.

"Come on, it's time for the fun part. I can't wait to see the shock on their faces," Trevor says as he starts up the stairs.

But I pause on the second step, turning Lucy to face me. "What does he mean by shock? I thought I was here because you already told them we were engaged?"

Trevor stops and turns around. "You didn't tell him what he was walking into? Oh, this is going to be good."

"Lucy, what am I missing?"

"They know we're engaged. They just didn't know you were coming." She winces.

"You fucking kidding me right now? Were you not going to warn me?" I'm whispering so Darryl doesn't hear and get suspicious, but there's enough venom in my voice to make it clear I'm angry.

"I was worried you'd back out. I'm sorry."

"You're sorry? Anything else you forgot to tell me, other than your parents have no idea I'm here and that you're rich as fuck?" I'm frustrated that I'm walking into an unknown situation without more time to prepare.

Another staff member, this one in an honest-to-God maid uniform, opens the front door, cutting our conversation short with no choice but to finish it later. And you can bet we will be.

"Greetings, Miss Lucy, Mr. Trevor. Your parents are waiting in the conservatory."

I feel like I'm in an actual twilight zone as we enter. If I thought the outside was grand, it's nothing compared to the opulent luxury once we step over the threshold. Completely over the top, absolutely indescribable, and with no subtlety that it's Christmas.

"Thank you, Mary," Lucy says to the woman as we walk by.

Trevor is in front of us, and I grab Lucy's hand, unsure if it's for her comfort or mine, considering I'm the one who should be on pins and needles at the moment.

As we weave through the extravagant house, I notice there's a fully decorated Christmas tree in each room we pass. We travel down a long corridor that descends into a large open area at the end with wall-to-wall windows, and a glass roof overlooking the ocean. Between us and the sand lies a pool that looks like it belongs at a resort.

Holy shit, who are these people?

"Lucy, dear. I'm so glad you made it. We were beginning to wonder if you'd changed your mind about coming." Her mom rises from the chair she was sitting in and stops short when she sees me. "Who do we have here?" she asks, her shrewd eyes glued to mine.

Lucy's dad places his book on the table beside him but stays seated, saying nothing while sipping the amber liquid in the glass he holds, waiting for an answer.

Trevor walks over to make himself a drink at the minibar and addresses me, giving his sister a few more precious seconds to gather her thoughts. "What do you want to drink? I think you might need it."

"I'll take a whiskey. Thanks," I respond before towing a petrified Lucy further into the room.

"Mr. and Mrs. Alcott, I'm Justin, Lucy's fiancé. It's a pleasure to be here. I apologize for barging in unannounced, but I surprised Lucy at the airport today. She thought I couldn't break free from work, but I made some last-minute changes to make it happen. I knew how important it was to Lucy for me to meet you."

"Surprise!" Lucy says, plastering on a fake smile as she holds up her hand, flashing the ring while Trevor brings my drink over.

She walks over to her mom, and sure enough, the woman thoroughly inspects it. Her smile upon completion is somewhat reassuring. They hug and air kiss on each cheek as if they were in France, which we may as well be since I feel like I'm in a foreign country right about now.

"I'm glad you're wearing it this time. That makes it official, I guess," her mom comments.

"Mom, Dad, this is Justin Burns, my fiancé. Justin, this is my mom, Josephine, and my dad, Franklin." She gestures to each of them, and that's my cue.

Her mom seems the safest place to start, so I shake her hand first. "Mrs. Alcott."

"What a nice surprise. We're happy to have you, Justin. We've been dying to meet the man who stole Lucy out from under us," she says in a way that makes me question whether she meant it as an insult.

Next is her dad, who rises from his chair as I approach. His handshake is much firmer, and the battle of wills is apparent. However, I'm not stupid enough to overpower him right out of the gate, so I relax my grip.

"It's good to meet you, sir. I'm sorry for showing up unexpectedly, but I was anxious to meet Lucy's family and put any concerns you have about me marrying your daughter to rest."

"We'll see if that's possible, Mr. Burns. It's interesting we didn't hear anything about you until last month… after you were already engaged. We have a lot to discuss while you're here."

"I'm sure we do. I'm prepared to earn your trust by answering any questions you have. Lucy's a remarkable woman, and I'm in love with your daughter, sir. I understand your apprehension about her future husband, but I assure you I'm the right man to stand by her side." My gaze doesn't leave his eyes as I make the statement I prepared on the way here.

"That's a nice speech, but I'll be the judge of that. In the meantime, you have a lot of ground to cover. Our acceptance of this marriage isn't to be expected but earned."

Their acceptance? What the fuck is his plan if they disapprove?

"Understood, sir." If this situation weren't fictional, I would have a much different response to this uptight asshole.

I avoid losing my cool thanks to Lucy, who seems to snap out of the fog she's been in and intervenes. "Sorry I didn't warn you. I was so excited when he showed up at the airport that I wasn't thinking clearly, and it never crossed my mind to let you know. We'd like to freshen up before dinner, so do you mind if I give Justin a tour as I show him to his room?" She links her arm with mine and pulls me toward the hallway.

"That's a good idea. Be down in an hour appropriately dressed," her mom orders as Lucy drags me away.

We don't make it far before Darryl appears out of nowhere. "Miss Lucy, I put you and Mr. Burns in the right-wing guest quarters. I assumed you would want your privacy," he informs us with a bow—something I don't think I'll ever get used to.

"Oh, okay. I guess that makes sense. Thanks, Darryl," she responds, dragging me onward. "See you all soon," she yells over her shoulder since we're already ten steps out of the room and booking it in the direction we came from.

"What does appropriate dress entail?" I ask Lucy, who's let me go but is still frantically rushing through the house. My arm darts out to stop her. "Whoa, slow down there."

"We have bigger issues to worry about than what clothes to wear. We're expected to sleep in the same room," she whispers in the foyer at the base of the stairs.

"What did you think was going to happen? We're adults who have been dating and are currently engaged to be married. Did they think you were saving yourself for marriage, or do you suppose they know we've *already done the deed*?" I whisper back, my words dripping with sarcasm.

"Ugh. You're so annoying. This wasn't part of the plan."

"No? What was part of the plan? Because I'm pretty sure you

didn't have one. You didn't tell them I was coming, Lucy. How did you think me not knowing that information was in your favor? What the fuck?"

"This is ridiculous." She puts her head in her hands. "Let's just go back in there and tell them the truth. It's not going to work anyway. I'm sorry I dragged you into this." She looks up at me, and the torment on her face is unmistakable.

I know the right thing to do would be what she suggested, but the stubborn side of me won't have it. I've made it this far— there's no way I'm quitting.

"Oh, no, you don't. I didn't just lie through my teeth in there to turn back now. We're sticking this out for better or worse, wifey, so you better give me that tour. Otherwise, I'll be lost forever in this palace." She groans, prompting me to continue, "I'll let the rest drop for now, but you have some explaining to do later." Boy, does she ever.

"Fine. I'll show you enough to navigate your way, but keep up because dinner is in an hour, and you can't be late around here." She avoids commenting on my last words.

After a thirty-minute tour, Lucy opens the door to our room. *Rooms* is more appropriate, and to say they're over the top is an understatement, which I've discovered applies to the entire place. A sizable sitting room greets us with a kitchenette and bar on one side. Opposite the door we entered, two stairs lower into a larger area housing a massive, oversized four-poster bed. The far wall is made entirely of glass, with a sliding door to the veranda over-looking the ocean. To the right is an en suite bathroom and larg-er-than-life walk-in closet, where the suitcases have already been emptied, our clothes hung and tucked away. The entire situation is extravagance at its finest.

"We only have twenty minutes to freshen up, so don't dally. I'll take the bathroom first." She grabs a dress from one of the hangers, and the door closes to the bathroom right as I'm about to ask what to wear.

Judging by her choice, it's formal, so I choose accordingly and change, deciding to give her space for now. When we return to the room later, there'll be plenty of time for answers.

7

NOT SO SILENT NIGHT

Lucy

WE SURVIVE DINNER UNSCATHED AND ARE FINALLY ON the way to our room, calling it a day with five more to go. Surprisingly, Trevor was a good buffer at dinner, keeping the conversation from taking a nosedive at any point by taking over when necessary. I wasn't expecting him to be so helpful after his animosity toward Justin at the airport, but he must have decided to save me from any more torture than necessary.

Mom and Dad drilled Justin about his business and made rude assumptions about its size and significance, but he did well to set them straight on all counts. He remained confident and poised throughout the entire inquisition. Justin's pride in his company showed as he spoke of all he's accomplished and the growth sustained since its inception.

He briefly discussed his service in the military, which I knew about, but further explained how it inspired him to pursue a career in security. He noticeably avoided his childhood, other than where he grew up, sticking to his more recent years. Although I'm curious about his past, my parents didn't seem fazed.

I'm sure Dad will dig deeper when he gets an opportunity for a one-on-one interrogation, but for now, Justin is holding his own, which is impressive for someone who walked into this blindly.

Speaking of, I'm dreading returning to our room where he'll finally have me alone and will no doubt drill me about my elusiveness. I've done so well avoiding scrutiny, but now that the cat's out of the bag, I'll have no choice but to come clean about everything. Well, not everything, but more than I want to.

Being put in the same room is an unfortunate situation. I still can't believe our sleeping arrangements didn't occur to me sooner. A pep talk from myself would have been excellent preparation for the awkwardness. While the butterflies in my stomach are about to burst free, Justin opens the door to our room, ushering me through.

To make matters worse, there's a printed schedule for the week waiting for us on the sitting room table, but on the flip side, there's a bottle of chilled champagne to congratulate the newly engaged couple.

"Thank God for small favors," I say as I unwrap the cork.

As expected, he doesn't waste any time jumping in while I open the bottle, which I'm sure can't do anything but help at this point. "An actual itinerary for the week? What the fuck, Lucy? Were you hoping I wouldn't notice the size of the house? The butler? There's a maid, for Christ's sake. Could you have at least given me a heads-up? I would've been more prepared and made sure to pack appropriately. Hell, maybe I wouldn't have looked shell-shocked and made an ass out of myself in front of your brother—who, by the way, already has it out for me, thanks to you."

"Nope, that's all thanks to you." The death glare he gives me as I hold out a glass for him is harsh. "Okay, that's not the point. Look, yeah, I probably should have prepared you a little more. It's not something I like to talk about. It's the main reason I stay as far away as possible from this place. And what does it matter? You'll be here a week and never see them again, so who cares?" Why does that bother me more than it should?

"I do. And you should, too, for that matter. I'm *your fiancé*. Although, according to your father, it sounds like I'll have to pass some crazy ass test if that means dick around here."

Yeah, he's angry. "Okay, so I didn't mention my family's wealth. And forgot to tell you that my parents weren't expecting you. Aaand, yes, I told my brother what an ass you are. But—"

"What an ass I *am* or *was*? Because I'm pretty sure I'm here saving yours." He downs his whole glass of champagne and holds it out for a refill. Maybe he'll soften up with one more.

"I guess we can call ourselves even then. Maybe. Or maybe not. We'll see after this week if you've worked up to that."

He sighs in frustration and retreats with his full glass to the closet. "I'm getting comfortable, and then we'll continue this conversation." A few seconds later, the door to the bathroom closes, giving me a much-needed reprieve.

I will admit, only to myself, that in hindsight, I may have made a few mistakes where Justin is concerned. However, in my defense, this is a unique situation. I mean, what if I told my parents and they said he couldn't come? What good would that have done? And where would we be if I hadn't told my brother the truth, and he saw right through us, as siblings tend to do, and ended up making this even more difficult?

Why is it that in the heat of an argument, I can never think on my feet to make a good case, but after, I'm chock-full of reason? *Ugh.*

How is this situation going to work? There's no way we can sleep in the same bed together. No, absolutely not. And before he gets any ideas, I'm taking control by making him a bed on the couch. That's precisely what I'm in the middle of doing when he finally emerges from the bathroom after what feels like an eternity and silences my muddled thoughts with the sight before me.

Gulp. I will myself to look away, but my eyes refuse. Dammit. He's shirtless. I mean, come on… he's purely fucking with me right now by putting his defined V on display right above his waistband. The sweats he's wearing aren't helping my panty-melting situation with their formfitting style that accentuates what I happen to know he's packing between those muscular thighs, which I'm also very familiar with.

"What are you doing, Lucy?"

Did his voice turn sultry, or did I drink too much? I look at my glass and see that it is indeed empty. It's for sure the champagne. My mind is playing tricks on me.

"Uh… getting your bed ready?" *Hmm.* Did that sound provocative? It certainly wasn't supposed to—unless it was my lady parts talking.

"That's funny because there's already a bed ready for me"—he points behind him—"right there."

Damn, all this talk of beds isn't good for me, but my mouth doesn't get the memo. "That's my bed. This is yours." I point down to the couch I've set up with blankets and a pillow.

"You expect my six-foot-four frame to sleep comfortably on

that less than six-foot couch? Hmm… I think the ginormous king will do just fine, but I appreciate your effort. Ready for a refill?" he says as he walks closer with his empty glass.

"What took you so long in there anyway?"

He looks at me pointedly. "You really want to know?"

Fucking champagne.

"Never mind. It's my turn. To use the bathroom, I mean, not the other thing." I hurry toward the bathroom.

"Let me know if you need any help."

"I'm locking the door, don't even think about it."

"Oh, I'll be thinking about it."

"Ugh." I stop at the closet to grab my pajamas, then head into the bathroom, locking the door immediately. No more champagne for me.

Justin

This is too much fun.

Taking care of myself was a necessary evil with what I knew was coming. There's no way I would have been able to lie next to Lucy and keep my cock under control. I'm not nearly satisfied, but at least taking the edge off will help because we *will* be sleeping next to each other—unless her stubbornness wins out.

Using sound reasoning, I fill my glass with more champagne, knowing it won't be good tomorrow, and who wastes hundred-dollar bottles of the good stuff? Certainly not me. With the glass in one hand and the schedule in the other, my legs carry me to the bed. Picking up my phone, I take some time to catch up on messages while waiting for Lucy. Work goes on without me since jobs are assigned to others, but I still need to be available for any major issues.

I'm still surprised dinner went as well as it did. Other than her father being an arrogant asshole, I'd say we made it through the first day unscathed. However, it could've gone even smoother if Lucy had been up-front with me about a few things. In fact, it's Lucy's turn for the third degree before we call it a day. If she thinks she's getting away with blindsiding me like this, she's got another thing coming.

The door to the bathroom opens, and Lucy materializes in front of me wearing Christmas pajamas with dancing reindeer saying, "All the jingle ladies." I can't stop myself from breaking out in laughter.

She looks down. "What? It's not that funny. And why are you in the bed?"

I pull myself together enough to answer, "No, it's not. This whole situation is, though."

"I guess that's one thing we can agree on. What we aren't in agreement on is the sleeping arrangement."

"You made up the couch. You can sleep on it. Or… you could try behaving like an adult, use the other half of this massive bed, and sleep comfortably. Besides, we're not done talking." I grab the covers opposite me and pull them down, patting the mattress.

"Let's not get started on the topic of behaving like an adult, or you'll be the one talking, and frankly, I don't want to hear it."

With that, she turns on her heels toward the sitting room and scoops up a blanket from the couch, bringing it back. She rolls it up the long way and sets it between us.

"There. That's the line. Not even one toe goes over it." She climbs into the bed, abruptly yanking the covers over her, crossing her arms defiantly with a huff.

"You're cute when you pout, you know that? I've never seen this side of you."

"You haven't spent enough time with me to see my many sides."

She looks down and grabs the paper next to her. "Do you want to go over the schedule, or what?"

The fucking schedule. What kind of family does that? There's a new surprise around every corner when it comes to Lucy and her world. I'd like to reduce the amount of them.

"First, start talking. What do I need to know before your dad corners me for this discussion we're supposedly having? It doesn't look good for either of us if it goes badly, so cut the crap with the secretive shit." I'm done playing nice guy until she gives a little in return.

She rolls her eyes before speaking. "Everything is about money to him. It's all he's ever cared about, so anything he says or asks will likely have to do with that. Job, future plans, background. He'll probably want to know how secure you are financially, and I'm sure there will be mention of a prenup. Just go along with whatever he says, and you should be fine. Like I said, after this week, none of it matters."

I nod my head in acceptance.

I'm not leaving anything to chance at this point. "Your mom bought our proposal story, but now she keeps trying to pin us down on wedding plans. Do we want to keep blowing it off or come up with something to appease her? I'd like the rest of the week to be less awkward than it was today, and that's only going to happen if we start communicating more."

"Okay, yeah, you're right. We should come up with something. But first, how about we pretend for a second that we are interested in each other and ask questions that we would ask a potential spouse? I'll go first. Do you want kids?"

My head jerks back at the turn in conversation. This wasn't quite where I thought she was going, but it's not a bad idea, so I'll roll with it. Except… "I don't know. I've never been asked that or even considered it."

"Well, you better decide—because I wouldn't say yes to marrying you if I didn't know."

"Do you want kids?"

"Yes. I want a boy and a girl just like me and my brother. The girl will be named Victoria, and the boy will be named Trevor after my brother."

"Ha. That's not happening. I'm not having my daughter teased her whole life. 'Oooh, Victoria… want to share your secret?' Absolutely not. I could get on board with Trevor, but only if we mend fences."

"Oh my God. You have no say since these aren't your children."

"Really? Should we let your mom know about this?"

She flings her hands up in frustration before snatching my glass of champagne, taking a big gulp and setting it down. "You're seriously impossible. Children or not, answer the question. Or do we agree on two?"

"I'm good with two, names debatable. My turn. You haven't changed your mind about Thailand for the honeymoon, have you? Because I'm all for it."

Her jaw drops as she looks at me. "You remembered?"

"Of course I did, baby. You…" I point to her, then bring my pointer fingers together before making a circle. "…complete me."

Grabbing the pillow behind her back, she whacks me with it while laughing. "You're awful."

Laughing along with her, I rip the pillow out of her hands and toss it on the floor. My hands reach for her hips and push her down before I climb on top, caging her in. "You. Are. Irresistible."

My lips crash to hers, and without hesitation, she kisses me back fervently, as if her life depends on it. And at this moment, it does because nothing could stop me from devouring her right here, right now.

My tongue battles for more, wanting what it's been denied for so long. It's like we were never apart with how familiar this feels. My hand winds its way into her hair and tugs, causing her to moan into my mouth, making my cock throb. I grind into her, looking for relief, but the second she feels me, her hands press hard on my chest and push me away.

"Stop. No, this isn't part of the plan. I may not have had one to begin with, but even if I did, this wouldn't be included."

Easing back, I can't help that the first thing I notice is her chest heaving up and down, making her breasts rise with every breath. At least I know she's just as into it as I am. Fuck, I didn't mean to move so quickly. My goal was to take it slow and slide back into the easiness between us. But fuck if I'm not just as powerless with her now as I was back then.

"I'm sorry. I didn't mean to do that." Rolling back to my side, I exhale loudly in frustration, partly at myself, but more so sexually. My cock is hard as a fucking rock and dying for another release. As easy as it would be to slink away and do just that, the more important thing to do is stay and make this right.

"I swear it wasn't my intention. While you were getting ready for bed, I specifically schooled myself to behave. But damn, I meant it when I said you were irresistible—"

She starts to cut me off, but I stop her by putting my hand up and continuing, "But… I promise I won't make another move—until you beg for it."

"That will not be happening."

"That's too bad."

"For you, maybe." She huffs and rolls over, facing away from me. "And in case you weren't paying attention to the schedule, we're expected at breakfast at nine tomorrow, followed by a visit to the Christmas tree farm to cut down our tree. So be ready."

"Oh, thank God, because the seven I've counted so far is laughable for a mansion this size," I say haughtily. Hearing her quiet giggle is pure satisfaction as I hit the light before closing my eyes, more content than I've been in months.

8

TRADITIONS

Lucy

"WHAT'S THE PLAN? STRAP THE TREE TO THE TOP?" JUSTIN motions to the custom-configured Escalade in which the five of us were chauffeured to the Christmas tree farm.

Rolling my eyes, I pull him along behind the rest of my family toward the office. "No, silly, we pay them to bring it to us after we cut it down."

He stops me halfway there. "Why exactly are we doing this?"

"It's tradition. We cut down our tree every year and then decorate it that night. This is my brother's and my favorite part of Christmas because it's one of the only times we're just a normal family… who wears ugly sweaters." She gestures to the attire we've all donned for the occasion. "The tree is never perfect, holds all our homemade ornaments, and is the one Santa leaves presents under."

"The Santa you don't believe in anymore? You could have told me about this tradition instead of your made-up Santa's milk and cookies story."

"It wasn't made-up, but we stopped doing it around seven years old after we learned the truth. Plus, it was worth it to see you stunned speechless," I tease, only to have Justin tickle me, causing uncontrollable laughter.

"Justin, stop!"

"I will for a kiss," he whispers in my ear.

"Justin," I plead between fits of laughter. Trying to twist from his hold is impossible.

"Come on, Lucy. One kiss. I won't even require tongue."

"Ugh, fine," I relent, not seeing any other way out.

He finally stops and gently brushes the hair from my face. With both hands framing my cheeks, he leans down and softly grazes his full lips against mine. It feels like heaven. Our mouths dance with each other until my tongue darts out for a taste, and he suddenly pulls back.

"Uh-uh. No tongue, remember?" He smirks.

I pull away and wipe my mouth. "Whatever. I was only doing it because you made me. I didn't even want to."

"So, that was just a slip of the tongue then?" he jests.

I groan in frustration and continue toward the rest of my family, not bothering to wait for him.

Last night, he said he wouldn't touch me again until I begged. That is *not* happening. The chemistry between us is intense, but I won't allow myself to fall for his charm again—I learned that lesson last time. Damn him and his kissable lips.

"You two looked pretty cozy over there," Trevor says quietly as he steps out of the office where our parents are checking in.

"Shut up."

He laughs before taking a serious tone. "He better not break your heart again, or I'll break him."

"Don't worry, it's not like that, trust me."

"Just be careful," he warns quietly while looking past me.

A few seconds later, Justin plops his arm on my shoulder. "Who's ready to have some fun?"

Trevor's pointed look says it all.

Justin

Yesterday was an experience like no other. Holidays with a rich as fuck family are truly something else. After decorating the tree, another formal dinner, and enough spiked eggnog to fill a trough, Lucy and I ambled to bed without any pretenses. I didn't even have the energy to try and get her worked up for me, which is my number one goal after my promise not to touch her until she begs.

However, with the busy schedule, it will be some time before I can focus on that. Unfortunately, my attention will be on her dad and brother this morning since golf is first on the agenda today.

"What would've happened if I'd never swung a club before? Does he not care if I can play or not?" I ask while finishing up in the bathroom. The door is open, and Lucy is leaning against the frame.

She shrugs. "If you don't golf, he won't approve of our marriage, so this is just another one of his tests."

"Great. So play well is what you're telling me?" I turn toward the doorway, fighting the temptation to kiss her.

"It doesn't really matter since we're not actually together.

You're taking this way too seriously." She rolls her eyes, and my willpower snaps.

My hand reaches for her hair, and I pull her head back to look up at me. "Would you rather I not give a fuck and cause your dad to disapprove of me? I'm sure he would be all too eager to bring Nathan in to take my place." I lean down to her neck and brush my nose along her jawline. "Is that what you want, Lucy?" My lips faintly skim her soft skin, causing her to moan.

"No… I want…" she starts to say with a whimper but trails off.

"Hm? What was that?" I whisper and nip her earlobe.

She's panting now, right where I want her. "Justin…"

"You can do it, baby. Tell me what you want."

"Justin, I—" A knock on the bedroom door causes her to jump back and stumble, catching herself on the dresser. She stares at me for a second and looks down at my raging hard-on.

"Coming," she yells while frantically combing through her hair with her fingers before opening the door to a smug-looking Trevor.

I don't hide while readjusting my swollen cock. Bastard should know what shitty timing he has.

"Hope I'm not interrupting anything, but it's time to go, and we need Justin." I haven't wanted to punch the smirk off someone's face this much in a long time.

"No. You're not. Perfect timing, actually. Justin just finished."

It's my turn to smirk at her choice of words. "I certainly wish I had."

Lucy groans and looks at Trevor. "That's not what I meant. We weren't doing anything, I swear."

I walk over to her with a look of admonishment. "Don't lie,

baby. Your brother can see right through you." Leaning down, I kiss her forehead before she shoves me away.

Lucy

"Sorry, sis. I know you wanted to take Justin around town today for some shopping, but we got a little carried away," my brother says as he and Justin stagger into the library together.

"Yeah, these guys thought I couldn't hold my own. I showed them," Justin slurs, leaning against the doorframe for support.

"It's fine. We can go tomorrow. Is it nap time, then?" I address them both.

"You just want to get me into bed, don't you?" Justin retorts. Both guys laugh.

"Okay then. I'll take that as a yes. Come on, big guy," I say to Justin as I thread my arm through his and tug him toward our room.

"Guess how many different golf-named drinks there are?" Justin asks in wonder.

"I'm gonna go out on a limb here and say too many."

"Fuck. You got it. Do you know how amazing you are?"

I'm shaking my head, grinning while pushing our door open to guide him inside.

"No, I mean it. You're incredible." He cages me against the door as soon as it closes behind us. "And beautiful, in case I haven't told you lately. And you're smart and funny, and you're just the whole goddamn package, Lucy."

He has no idea what he's saying, and if I don't stop him, he'll regret this the minute he sobers up. The last thing I want is for the rest of this visit to be awkward, which means it's time to move.

I sneak out from under his arms so quickly that he almost

tumbles trying to stop me. "If you nap now, we might still have time to do something before dinner. Why don't you get into bed, and I'll shut the blinds."

"I'll only nap if you lie with me."

"That's not a good idea." Picturing myself in bed with him after the incident this morning makes me hot. I can't believe how close I was to giving in and asking him to kiss me.

"I completely disagree."

"Of course you do."

"Come on, Lucy. You know you want to."

How can his voice be that sexy while he's three sheets to the wind? I'm moving toward the bed, my feet taking over. He probably won't give up, so I'm only prolonging the inevitable by arguing. I'll wait until he passes out, which I bet won't take long.

"I'll lie down, but no funny business. I mean it," I say sternly while a smile slowly spreads across his face.

"We'll leave our clothes on. Just be next to me." He climbs in and holds his arm out for me to join him.

So, I do.

He wraps his arm around me, lifting my upper body onto his chest. His sigh of contentment is contagious. As predicted, he's out within a minute. My body melts into his as if it were always meant to be there. It's already difficult trying to stay angry with him, and when he's so sweet and feels this good, it's nearly impossible.

Justin

Her smell infiltrates my senses. It's the first thing to register as I regain consciousness, along with the satisfaction of holding Lucy in my arms again. I'm afraid to open my eyes and discover I'm dreaming, so I don't. Instead, I relish the feel of her while taking in the moment. My mind starts to recall how we ended up here, making me smile at the memory of our banter and how adorable she is trying to fight this pull between us.

Confident I'm not in a dream, I peel open my eyes to see Lucy sleeping peacefully, her head resting on my chest and full lips parted in slumber. Remembering why I let her go all those months ago is becoming harder to recall and even harder to forgive myself for. It's not fair to fault her for holding back after the way I handled things.

It was an awful moment in time for me, and my actions had dire consequences. Basically, I made a bad situation worse and have paid the price ever since. I want her back, but not because of some sob story excuse. No, she needs to want me, mistakes and all, because there's no guarantee I won't fuck up again.

This is my chance to right the wrongs I've committed and redeem myself—if she'll let me. Her walls seem to be coming down little by little. I'm certainly more hopeful than I was a few days ago, and I think it's time to take things a step further.

My hands begin slowly caressing her. One on her back, up and down, while the other moves to her face, tucking the hair behind her ears. She shifts her body and moans, causing blood to flow directly south. My arm snakes further down her back to her ass, feeling her soft curves, and my head lowers to her temple to feel her skin against my lips.

She sighs in satisfaction, giving me the green light to proceed. Lifting her chin, my lips find hers, and before I realize what I'm doing, I roll her onto her back and climb on top of her. Desperate to be even closer, I use her ass to pull her further into me as I kiss her neck.

"God, Lucy. You feel so good, baby." My pelvis grinds into her, and we both moan at the friction.

I hit the sweet spot just behind her ear, and she rocks into me as she whimpers. My hand moves between her legs, and she instinctively opens them for me.

"Fuck. I need to see you come, baby. Will you let me do that for you?"

"Yes. Oh God, please."

I'll take that as her begging.

"Good girl." My hand dips into her waistband, under her panties, finding her drenched.

"Damn, sweetheart, if you needed me this badly, all you had to do was ask. I've been dying to get my hands on this pussy for days now." My fingers probe her hole, anxious to sink further.

"Justin…"

"Do you need me to fuck you with my fingers, baby? Do you want me to ram this tight pussy with my hand and make you scream?"

Her cry is the only answer I need, so without a word, I plunge two digits into her wet heat and revel in the feel of her channel sucking me in. My arm strains from the pressure I'm applying as my fingers flick her inner walls. She screams in ecstasy as my lips continue their assault on her neck while thrusting into her. My swollen cock is humping her leg like a dog, searching for release.

"I know you need this, baby. You want to be fucked so bad, don't you?"

I grab her hair and pull, her feral gaze meeting mine when I raise my head.

"You're going to look at me while I make you come. No one makes you come like I do. Isn't that right?"

"No." She shakes her head as much as possible with my grip on her hair.

"That's right. Let me have it, then. Come for me."

I pull her hair harder, find her G-spot, and she fucking explodes. Her tight pussy squeezes my fingers, pulsing as she screams her release.

My mouth descends, my tongue plunging into her mouth as my hips maintain their thrusting.

In the blink of an eye, I'm on my knees, unzipping my pants to finish myself while my other hand continues to milk her pleasure. I pump my cock furiously. Once, twice, three times, and I come on top of her stomach, marking her as mine.

"Fuck. Oh God, Lucy. Damn, your pussy feels so good." I grunt my release until the very last drop before sinking back on my ass, slowly removing my hand from between her legs.

"Holy shit, that was incredible," I say after catching my breath.

"Yeah. Good." She pants each word in between breaths.

9

HO, HO, HO

Justin

"MERRY CHRISTMAS EVE," I SAY THE MOMENT LUCY'S EYES blink open. I've been watching her sleep for the last fifteen minutes, remembering how nice it was to have her in my arms for most of yesterday. Having staff bring food to the room is a nice perk of the Alcott residence. After our late afternoon nap, we ended up staying in bed the rest of the night watching movies.

"Merry Christmas Eve." She smiles softly.

"Should we celebrate?" I raise my eyebrows in question.

"No. We should get our last-minute shopping done. The stores close early today, and it's your fault we didn't go yesterday."

"I'm not taking the blame for that. It was your brother's fault for plying me with drinks, and then yours for being so damn irresistible."

I pull her into me and start tickling her sides—one of my favorite things to do—so I can hear her laugh.

The next thing I know, her mouth is on mine, taking me off guard, but it doesn't stop me from taking advantage of the moment. Within seconds, we're moaning and grinding into each other before she abruptly pushes me away.

"Don't distract me. Seriously, we need to get going." She looks at the clock on the nightstand. "We're leaving in thirty minutes."

"I can be ready in five. Let's use the other twenty-five wisely." Reaching for her, I'm met with another shove.

"Well, I need all thirty, so you're on your own," she retorts as she climbs out of bed.

"You're going to make me use my hand again?" I call out while she's in the closet.

As she exits, Lucy pauses with a hand on her jutted hip and smirks. "Hate to break it to you, but that's all you'll be using while you're here."

"Come closer and say that again," I challenge.

"Not a chance. See you in"—she looks at her bare wrist

—"twenty-five." Then she walks into the bathroom, locking the door behind her.

I roll onto my back and groan.

"You never did tell me how yesterday went." Her hand covers her mouth to muffle the full bite of burger she just took, garbling her speech. We've been shopping for a few hours and decided to break for lunch.

I can't keep from laughing. "Geez, didn't your parents teach you manners?"

She swallows dramatically. "Oh please, they shoved them down my throat so much, I was done for."

I chuckle at her response. "Good to know." She's the complete opposite of what you would expect to come from this family.

"Now spill, how'd it go?" she asks while stuffing a fry into her mouth.

"Well, your dad insisted I ride in his cart and continued to drill me about my business aspirations throughout the day. He asked about my intentions with you. I mean, I thought that was obvious, but it seems he was referring to getting my hands on your money. Which was interesting, since I didn't know you had any." I narrow my eyes in accusation.

"Hmm… yeah. I figured it was bound to come up eventually. He likes to hold that over my head."

"It wouldn't have anything to do with why you asked me to do this, would it?" The funny thing is it wouldn't matter. I can tell she doesn't have a pretentious bone in her body, but who wouldn't want to ensure their trust fund is secure?

"No, it didn't, I swear. I don't care about any of it. I don't want this lifestyle. I'd give it all up in a heartbeat if it meant I didn't have to answer to them anymore. That's why I asked you to do this. They shouldn't be dictating who I can and can't be with. Why do you think I moved across the country and took a job as a receptionist?"

I wouldn't know because she's never spoken about her family life. Not that I have any room to talk. I suppose we all have our hang-ups.

"Looks like they're still doing a pretty good job of it regardless of your address." She's delusional if she thinks otherwise.

"I don't care. I'm done with all that." *Delusional it is.*

"Nice try." I chuckle. "If that were true, I wouldn't be here."

Lucy

Damn him and his single eyebrow raise. He's right, but he doesn't have to be so smug about it. So instead of responding, I take another huge bite of burger and point to my mouth, indicating the inability to speak. *See? I have manners.*

"Lucy?" My name comes from an oddly familiar voice, and I snap my head to the right, mouth still full, to see my ex-boyfriend from high school. *Oh my God.*

My eyes widen as I gulp down the unfinished bite so I can speak. "Richard?"

"Holy shit. I thought that was you. Wow. It's been like, what— eight years?" he asks, reaching me and holding his arms out for a hug.

I stand to do so, only to hear a distinctly loud throat clear behind me. I step back right away to see Justin standing, looking every bit his six foot four.

"Justin, this is Richard, an old friend from high school. Richard, this is Justin."

"Her fiancé," Justin adds, sizing Richard up. *Crap.*

"You're engaged. That's… great. Congratulations are in order, I guess," Richard says as he leans forward for another hug, but Justin sticks his hand out to shake before he makes it.

"Nice to meet an old friend of Lucy's. Sorry, she didn't mention you. You went to school together?" *Oh, he's so sly.*

Trying to prevent an answer, I laugh awkwardly to interrupt.

"It's crazy running into you like this. Are you home for the holidays?" I ask Richard, effectively changing the subject.

"I am. It's about the only time I can get away from the office these days," Richard answers.

"Did you become an attorney like you always wanted?"

"Yeah, in fact, I just became the youngest partner in our firm," he boasts.

"That's amazing. You always were driven. I knew you'd make it big," I say genuinely.

"Thanks, Lucy. How about you? Where did you end up with your MBA from Harvard?"

"How did you know I got my MBA?"

"Lucy, our parents are friends. I ask about you occasionally."

I look at Justin, who seems pretty interested in where the conversation is going. He doesn't know any of this, and I'm pretty sure I'm in too deep to stop now.

"I wanted a change of scenery, so I ended up moving to California." No need to elaborate and tell him I'm just an assistant.

"No shit. Where at? I'm in Oceanside," he says hopeful.

"That's wild. I'm in San Diego."

"What are the odds we live within an hour of each other?" Richard asks.

"What are the odds?" Justin adds sarcastically.

All right, looks like it's time to wrap this up. What's the deal anyway? It's not like we're really engaged…

"It was good to see you, Richard. Congratulations on becoming partner. Tell your parents I said hi and Merry Christmas." That should be sufficient. I feel like I've covered all the bases.

"Yeah, same. Let me get your number, and if I'm in the area, the three of us can grab a drink or something," he says, handing me his phone to add my contact.

"Sounds good." For some reason, my palms are sweating, and guilt starts creeping up. After I'm done, I hand the phone back with a forced smile.

"I'll text you so you'll have my information. It was so great to see you, Lucy. Justin, it was nice to meet you. You've got an amazing girl here. Take care of this one," Richard says.

"Don't worry, I plan on it," comes his gruff reply.

Waving as Richard walks away, I sit back down to a scowling Justin. I'm not sure what his problem is, so I plop another fry in my mouth and wait.

"I take it 'old friend' means boyfriend. How long did you two date?"

"Does it matter? It was eight years ago."

"I'm just curious. You know, most people who get engaged talk about their past relationships at some point while they're dating."

"See, that's the thing about us. We never had the chance to get that far since someone here disappeared, so don't lecture me on what people do while they're dating. By the way—we're not actually engaged. You only have a few more days until none of this matters anyway."

"Have you not realized that it does matter? If you haven't guessed, I'm not only here to help you out, Lucy. I'm here because I want a second chance." He grabs my hand and holds it on the table, but I don't respond, unsure what to say.

Things have been heating up between us, but it didn't occur to me that he was in it for more than sex at this point. I figured there was some reason he didn't want to be with me all those months ago, and nothing has changed since then, not to mention my family would send anyone running for the hills. I'm reasonably sure Justin doesn't need money, so that's not it.

"Why?" It's all I've got.

He drops his head and shakes it. "I hate that you even have to ask, but I get it. Lucy, you're amazing, and I'm sorry I made you feel differently. You weren't the reason I walked away. If I could go back and change how that all went down, I'd do it in a heartbeat. What I need you to know is that you are the complete package, and everything I could ever want by my side. Will you give me the chance to redeem myself?"

"I'm not sure. I don't know if I can trust you again. I won't rule out a friends-with-benefits arrangement, but I'm not ready to commit to a relationship."

He smiles. "I can accept that. I'll keep working toward the latter, but I'll ensure you're satisfied with the benefits in the meantime." He wiggles his brows. "But for now, why don't you tell me about this MBA from Harvard."

"Wow, these are…" Instead of finishing his thought, Justin laughs as he holds up the pair of pajamas he just opened, which have a picture of Santa saying, "I do it for the hos."

My parents included him in our Christmas Eve tradition of gifting everyone a new pair. The problem is my brother handled the shopping this year since my parents were too busy—yeah, right. He bought Mom and Dad basic holiday-themed ones while humbly buying himself a pair that says, "Might as well sleep under the tree, 'cause we all know I'm the gift in the family."

"Nice one, Trevor. Are you calling me a ho?" I ask, referring to Justin's while laughing.

"I don't know… You're last, so go ahead and open yours," he answers cryptically.

I tear into mine and immediately start laughing. Since Trevor knew Justin would be here, it makes sense that he had ours tie in together. Mine say, "Santa's favorite ho."

Holding them up to show everyone, Justin loses it, practically crying from laughing so hard, which sets me off too, followed by everyone else. Soon, we're all wiping tears from our eyes. I haven't seen my parents laugh like this in a long time—it's nice.

After we calm down, my brother says, "All right, let's all change into them before the movie. We'll meet in the theater in twenty."

Justin rises and grabs my hand to help me up from the couch before leading us to our room.

I'm halfway to the closet when Justin swiftly tackles me to the bed, making me squeal. He lays me flat on my back, straddling me, trapping my arms above my head, my new pajamas thrown to the side.

"How's my favorite ho feeling?" He nips my ear.

I giggle. "Much better now," I respond while he works my neck with his mouth, turning my giggles into moans.

"Good. We have twenty minutes… Whatever shall we do?"

"What you're doing is good." My neck is straining to give him more room to roam.

"Oh, we can do better than this. Why don't I help you get changed?" His hands reach for the hem of my shirt, slowly lifting it while skimming his thumbs along my skin, leaving behind a trail of goose bumps.

I hum in agreement. "Okay."

"I love you being so agreeable." He scoots down and grazes my belly with featherlight kisses as he removes my shirt.

Eager for more, I reach back to undo my bra, flinging it to the floor. "I don't wear a bra with pajamas."

"Is that so? Good thing you took it off then." His mouth immediately engulfs my breast while circling my nipple with his tongue.

"I could stay here all night and suck these beautiful tits, but we're short on time, so I better finish getting you ready for your pajamas."

"Mm-hmm. You should, for sure."

His mouth moves back down my stomach as he undoes my pants and pulls them down, leaving my panties in place, but then he pauses and glances up.

"Maybe you should put some fresh panties on to go with your new pajamas?"

"That's exactly what I was thinking."

Justin winks. "Great minds think alike."

Within seconds, all my clothes are on the floor, and Justin's face is between my legs, his hands spreading me wide open for him.

"Fuck, Lucy, you smell like heaven." He licks up my center. "And you taste like dessert. Goddamn, baby, I need to feast on you."

Before I know what's happening, he rolls us over so he's flat on his back, me on top of him, then drags me up so I'm sitting on his torso, my core inches from his mouth.

"Justin, what are you doing?"

"I want you to sit on my face and let me eat that pussy while you get yourself off. Scoot yourself on up here."

"You can't be serious."

"Get your pussy up here right now, Lucy. If I have to ask you again, you won't like the consequences." He slaps my ass, causing me to jerk forward on my knees.

Taking advantage of my movement, he pulls me right down over his face, making me grab onto the headboard for support. And oh God… his tongue rams into my hole and starts flicking vigorously while he cups my ass, pulling me tighter against him. I can't stop the moans from escaping.

My pelvis starts rocking over his mouth of its own accord. His thumb finds my clit and begins circling it while he continues lavishing me with his tongue. I'm seconds from coming when his other hand squeezes my breast and pinches my nipple.

"Justin, oh God, I'm coming. Fuck—oh God, oh God." He pinches harder. "JUSTIN!" I flood his mouth with my release while his moans assure me he's enjoying this as much as I am as I ride it out, continuing to slide back and forth until the very last pulse. A moment later, I collapse, letting myself slump to the bed beside him.

"That was fucking hot," he says with a sigh. He almost sounds as content as I am.

"Damn, I forgot how good at that you are."

"That was all you, baby. All I did was enjoy my dessert."

"We do have a few minutes left, maybe—"

"Nope. Time to head to the theater."

"But—"

"Don't worry, Lucy. Tomorrow's Christmas, and I know exactly what I want."

10

JINGLE ALL THE WAY

Justin

CHRISTMAS DAY WENT OFF WITHOUT A HITCH. WE concocted a plan to explain that Lucy and I were having our gift exchange once we returned home. Other than that, I bought her a scarf and a pair of earrings I came across while out shopping the other day, and she gifted me a button-down dress shirt. For her parents, I gave her dad a very nice bottle of scotch, and Lucy helped me choose a pair of earrings for her mom.

Dinner was about as pleasant as usual. Her dad still hasn't warmed up to me, but other than that, it was an easy, relaxing day with plenty of cocktails throughout.

We're sitting at the dinner table when her dad addresses me directly for the first time. "Justin, I think it's time you and I sit down and talk before you go. Meet me in my office tomorrow morning at eleven o'clock."

"Good idea, Mr. Alcott. Looking forward to it." What else can I say—that it's the last thing I'd like to do on my final day here? Not happening, but it's certainly what I'm thinking.

"Great." He immediately moves on. "Also, we're having some friends join us for dinner tomorrow evening. After hearing Lucy was in town, the Siemens insisted on seeing her before she leaves."

"Really, Dad? Why didn't you ask me first? We already ran into Richard while shopping yesterday. I don't think dinner is necessary," Lucy protests.

Ah… Richard's family. Seriously? Richard Siemen?

I lean over to Lucy and whisper in her ear, "You dated someone named Dick Siemen?" She giggles and shoves me with her shoulder.

Not surprisingly, her dad rebukes her comment. "At his parents' request, yes, I do think it's necessary. They said they've missed you. You were practically family for over three years." Lucy rolls her eyes at her dad's comment.

Three years? This wasn't just some boyfriend—he was her fucking high school sweetheart. Dick probably took her virginity, for fuck's sake. Damn, I hate the guy more now than I already did.

Lucy looks to Trevor. "You'll be there, right?"

"Sorry, sis. It's my annual night after Christmas with the guys from school. You know that."

"Ugh. You suck," she pouts.

"Well, I'm certainly looking forward to it. I miss their family. Remember, we used to have so much fun… It hasn't been the same since you two parted ways," her mom adds to the irritating conversation.

"Getting to know one of Lucy's ex-boyfriends will be great.

Maybe he can tell me what not to do. Huh, honey?" I interject smoothly.

This earns me a death glare from Lucy, which makes me laugh. My hand reaches for her leg and gives her a reassuring squeeze. Everything will work out the way it's supposed to.

"I can't believe he did that. He's doing it to fuck with you, I'm sure. God, I'm sorry," Lucy says as we're sitting on the couch in our room with a glass of wine before we call it a night. However, calling it a night isn't what's going to happen if I have anything to say about it.

"Don't be sorry. I'm having fun coming up with all the different ways I'll be able to give him shit about his name."

"Don't. It's not his fault his parents were idiots. I mean, I love them, don't get me wrong, but come on… who names their kid that? Do you think it occurred to them at the time?"

"How could it not? They're just cruel if you ask me. But here's the question I have—was Dick the first to put his Siemen in you?"

"Oh my God. Shut up!"

"Oh, so he was then. I can hear his dirty talk now… Oh, baby, you—"

"STOP—just stop. That's terrible."

"I'll tell you what's terrible…" I set my glass on the table and lean into Lucy, sweeping her hair back so I can whisper into her ear. "I'll be limited to using the word 'cock' from now on." My hand pulls her hair, lifting her head to access her neck. "Like when I say,

'Get on your knees and take out my cock because I'm ready for my Christmas present now.'"

Her panting is sexy as hell, making her chest rise and fall, showing me she's just as excited for what's coming next. So does seeing her slide off the couch onto her knees before me. The flash of heat in her eyes signals no hesitation and causes my cock to harden even more in eager anticipation.

"I'd like you to do the unwrapping. Start with you first. I want to see those pretty tits bounce while my cock is down your throat." Her moan is almost enough to make me throw in the towel and rush this along, but driving her desire higher is equally enticing.

Watching Lucy slowly lift the sweater over her head makes me frantic with need. She deliberately removes her clothes at a leisurely pace, letting her bra straps gently glide down her arms until finally letting it fall to the ground. Damn, it hits me again how fucking perfect she is. I'm not sure how I got so lucky the first time or why I've been given a second chance, but I'm vowing not to screw this up again.

I can't wait a second longer, or my zipper will bust. "All right, baby. Time to unwrap my package." My hips flex, grabbing her attention.

Lucy

Thank God. The bulge in his pants has been tempting me all night, and after being taken care of twice already with no reciprocation on my part, I want to make sure he gets exactly what he needs. Justin starts undoing the buttons on his shirt one by one while I work his pants open. His torso is a work of art, and I can't help but drool as each inch is revealed, reminding me how lucky I am to have access to this beautiful specimen.

He lifts his hips and helps me lower his pants as his erection springs free, bobbing in front of my face. My mouth waters, and I lick my lips in anticipation. He's very well-endowed. We better be going all the way tonight, because I'm not sure how much longer I can wait before jumping the man myself.

His cock twitches. "He missed you, baby." Justin grabs his length, firmly stroking it up and down. "Tell me, did you miss him too?"

It's not difficult to answer. "Yes. I really did."

"Good. Prove it then and show me."

He angles himself toward my face as I rise to my knees and lean down to take him into my mouth. I open wide as he slides to the back of my throat, caressing my cheek with his thumb as my mouth takes over. Justin lets out a hiss, telling me he likes it.

"Fuck, Lucy, that feels so good. I forgot how deep you take me."

He thrusts his hips, plunging further, and I swallow him down, causing him to groan when he feels my throat muscles tighten around his length. My head rises slowly, sucking and licking along the way until I lift off with an audible pop and look at him with a seductive smile. I lick the head, dipping my tongue into the slit, causing his hips to jerk.

"You're such a tease. Keep it up, and I'll be running the show instead."

"Be my guest."

"Lucy… don't tempt me."

I hum in contemplation as I return my attention downward and take him in again. After a few minutes of devotion, his grunting becomes more intense, and I slow down, keeping him on the edge.

"You're asking for it, aren't you, baby? You know I'll fuck the tease right out of you. Is that what you want?" He fists my hair and tugs slightly so my eyes make contact with his.

My answering moan is enough for Justin to know it's exactly what I want.

"All right, sweetheart. I gave you fair warning. There's no going back now. Keep that mouth wide open for me."

His hand tightens its grip as his other hand grabs my head and presses me down completely, holding me there momentarily before allowing me to come up for air and repeating the movement again. God, I love when he's in control. My core clenches with desire, and if I weren't caught up in trying to breathe and not gag, my hand would be taking care of myself. As it is, all my focus is needed up here.

"You deep throat me so good, baby, but fuck, I need to come. I can't hold back, sweetheart. Fuck."

Holding my head still, he begins aggressively pumping his hips up and down in short, shallow thrusts while grunting in pleasure. My hands have a death grip on his thighs.

"Oh yeah. That's it. Breathe, baby. Breathe through your nose while I use that sweet mouth of yours. Fuck, yeah, just like that."

His cock seems to swell even more when he suddenly plunges deep and holds, pulsing, shooting his release down my throat, making me choke.

He grunts and talks through his release. "God, yes. That's right, take it. Swallow everything I give you. Fuck, fuck, fuuuck." When the last drop is spent, he pulls out, finally allowing me to suck air into my lungs.

His thumb wipes the drool and cum from my mouth while he looks down endearingly. "Holy shit, baby. Your mouth is a thing of wonder. That was the best present ever."

"I can think of a better one."

He laughs. "Is that so? What if I want to prolong the surprise?" His left eyebrow raises in challenge.

Looks like I'm taking things into my own hands. Rising to stand, I give him a smoldering look as he smirks at me. I'm not sure whether he's pushing me on purpose or serious about waiting, but either way, I'm going for it. I grab both breasts and squeeze seductively a few times before slowly lowering my hands to the top of my pants, pushing them down while leaving my sexy lace G-string on.

Justin's cock shows no sign of the orgasm he had five minutes ago and looks painfully ready to go again. His hand slides down to stroke himself leisurely while his eyes remain locked on the show in front of him.

I reach into my panties, making him groan. "Fuck, baby, tell me you're still on birth control. You know what happens when you tease me."

"I am," is the only response I give as I turn around, giving Justin my back.

Very slowly, I slide my panties down, bending over as I lower them to my ankles. There's rustling behind me, telling me I'm not the only one disrobing. Completely bared and on display, I remain bent over while my fingers reach back to tease my opening, feeling the moisture there, knowing it will drive him wild. I smile at Justin's growl, then squeal when he grabs me and brings me down on his lap.

"What did I tell you, baby? Play with fire, and you get burned."

"Why, Mr. Burns… didn't you know? I'm a pyromaniac."

"Then aren't you just fucking perfect for me."

He lowers his hips while propping me up with his thighs at the same time he lines himself up, giving no pause before he plunges in, pulling me down hard, his entire length impaling me.

I gasp at the intrusion, with a lustful moan following immediately behind. "Oh my God, Justin."

"Fuck, baby, you needed that, didn't you?"

"Yes. Please, more." This is exactly what I needed. I'll never be satisfied with anyone else. No wonder I barely tried. He literally ruined me for all others.

"Oh, I have so much more for you. Goddamn, Lucy, you're so fucking tight. Ride me hard. Bounce up and down on my cock."

With his help, I do just that. His hands lift me up and down rapidly while he thrusts deeper with each slam of my hips. His grunts blend with my gasps as we seek our pleasure together.

"Touch yourself, baby. Come all over my cock. I want you gushing."

It feels so good backward like this. The angle seems to hit something I've never felt before. The instant I touch my clit, my core clenches.

"Oh, fuck, that's it. Squeeze my cock. Keep doing that."

The next thing I know, there's pressure at my back door. I'm so wet his finger slides around my tight hole easily, and surprisingly, it feels good but scary at the same time.

I'm whimpering. "Justin? What are you doing?" The question comes out in pants.

"Your ass was feeling left out back here, baby. It'll feel so good, I promise. Just relax and keep focusing on that pussy for me, okay?"

I do, but then tense up the second he applies more pressure.

"Relax, sweetheart. I won't hurt you. Let me in, okay?" He barely pushes the tip of his finger in. "That's it, good girl."

After breaching my tight hole, he stills before applying more pressure and slides it in further. I'm not sure about it feeling good, but it's not terrible, so I continue massaging my clit, hoping to make it back to my pending climax. It seems like forever until instead of pushing, he changes direction and begins to slowly withdraw his finger. Suddenly, the floodgates open to the most intense pleasure I've ever experienced.

The scream that escapes is unstoppable. "Justin! Oh my God. Oh my God. What… Wait, oh God…"

"I know, baby. Let it go. Give in and come for me. Let me have it."

My orgasm hits me like a ton of bricks, my body convulsing while crying out my pleasure. One finger becomes two while he picks up speed and force, sending me into an abyss that doesn't seem to have an end in sight. Behind me, I hear Justin reach his own climax but am too caught up in mine to pay attention, his sounds flowing around me.

"Goddammit, Lucy. Fuck yeah. Oh fuck, baby, I'm filling you so full. Fuuuck."

His fingers retreat, practically sending me into another wave of pleasure as they slide out. I'm utterly spent, slumping forward, holding myself up with my hands on his knees. We never even made it to the bed.

"Come here, sweetheart." He pulls me back into his chest, both of us panting, coming down from our highs. His cock slowly starts shrinking, slipping out of me before he brings my legs up, turning my body so I'm cradled in his lap like a baby.

Contentedness like I've never felt before takes over my body, and I bask in our postcoital bliss.

11

THE LAST SUPPER

Justin

'LL ADMIT, I'M A LITTLE TIRED AFTER OUR MARATHON sexcapade last night. Not that I'm complaining. However, as I make my way to the office for my meeting with Mr. Alcott, it's hard not to visualize all the ways Lucy and I reacquainted ourselves with each other. Our chemistry is mind-blowing. There's never been anyone quite like Lucy, in or out of the bedroom. This feeling that we're meant to be together grows stronger each day.

Which is why this conversation with her dad is more important to me than she realizes. Despite this starting as a sham, I'd like us to move toward it becoming a reality. It's too soon for marriage, but I'm serious enough that it's time for her dad to accept our relationship.

Rather than wait for him to control the conversation, I start speaking as soon as I'm seated in one of the wingback chairs facing the desk. "Before we get started, I want to thank you again for welcoming me at the last minute. Lucy told me how our engagement was revealed at Thanksgiving, and I'm sorry it didn't happen more formally. We were waiting to make an announcement, hoping to savor our relationship for a while longer."

"It was certainly a shock to hear that our only daughter intends to marry someone we've never met, let alone heard about. I'm sure she told you our reaction was less than pleasant."

"To be expected, sir."

"Words were said in shock and anger. Those words, however, were not out of turn. Everything spoken was fact, and I will not waver in my decision."

I manage to keep a straight face as I respond, "A lot was said. I'd appreciate it if you could enlighten me on the exact part you're referring to."

"I'd be delighted. Lucy has a sizable trust fund that, if released, would allow her to be set for life and ensure the next generation is very well cared for. We made it clear to Lucy, and now I'll do the same for you. We expect her to marry within her class. Whoever she marries must meet our standards for us to relinquish the amount of money we're talking about. And I'm sorry to inform you, Mr. Burns, but you do not."

I'm trying my best to remain calm as I take in this new information that Lucy conveniently left out of her explanation. I'm dumbfounded that there are actual people in the world like this. To prohibit your daughter from marrying for love because of money is incomprehensible to me. Yet, here I am, faced with it, nonetheless.

"Let me make sure I understand. You've deemed me unworthy of your daughter, and because of that, you'll withhold her trust and—what, disinherit her? Does it not matter that we're in love?

That I treat her like she walks on water and am more than capable of providing for her and any family we decide to have?"

"There's more to life than love. We haven't worked this hard to amass wealth to see it squandered away."

"Then it might interest you to know that I have my own money, and plenty of it. In fact, we won't need a dime of her trust to live the life she's accustomed to. If that was your concern, you can put it to rest right now."

"It's more than money, Mr. Burns, I assure you. I won't tolerate a child who has no plans to continue the legacy we've created with someone of our pedigree by their side. You must understand that Lucy comes from a world beyond what you can achieve in this lifetime. It's nothing personal."

"What a relief." Sarcasm drips from my tone. "I'm glad we had this discussion. It was enlightening, to say the least. You'll understand when I politely tell you to fuck off."

"Understand or not, I'd like you to remember what you're asking of her by marrying you. Are you prepared to drive a wedge between Lucy and her family? And while she might be willing to say goodbye for *love*, someday, perhaps when children are involved, she might regret that decision. Are you willing to take that risk, Mr. Burns?"

"We're done here." I stand and start toward the door.

"Take some time to think about it before making a rash decision. And Justin?" I stop and turn around, making eye contact with the bastard, hoping he sees the murder in my gaze. "Maybe dinner tonight will help shed some light on the matter. You might understand what I'm talking about."

His final words sting as I leave the office and walk through the house. I see red, taking in my surroundings through a new lens, hating the arrogant wealth and everything it stands for.

There's no way I can see Lucy right now. I need time to process and figure out how to handle this situation. After last night, my mind was made up to make Lucy part of my future. Now? I'm not so sure what the right move is. She told me she didn't want her family's money, but does she understand it's all or nothing? Her entire relationship with her parents rests in my hands.

Coming outside for air, I walk to the edge of the pool deck and face the ocean, pondering my options and the consequences of each one. My anger is doing me a disservice by causing irrational thoughts, but regardless, I need to blow off this steam on my own.

While I know that, unfortunately, Lucy does not.

She walks up beside me and ducks under my arm, leaning into me and laying her head on my chest. "There you are. I've been looking for you since I saw my dad and knew you were done talking. Have you been out here since?"

"Yeah, just taking in the view. It's crazy we haven't been out here more. It's beautiful."

"It is. Growing up here desensitizes you to it, but you're right. Do you want to go for a swim? We haven't done that yet, and it's our last day." She looks up at me with puppy dog eyes that I can't resist.

"That's exactly what I want to do."

Hours later, I can tell my mood is starting to wear on Lucy. I've been out of sorts since meeting with her dad this morning, and while she has no idea what he said to upset me like this, I'm not inclined to tell her.

We had fun swimming and horsing around in the pool. Thankfully, I was able to escape my thoughts for a little while, but there was no hope of keeping them at bay when we returned to our room to get ready for dinner. Lucy definitely noticed, especially since we had plenty of time, yet I made no attempt to get in her pants.

"Hey, what's going on with you? You've been weird ever since that talk with my dad. What did he say to put you on edge? You know it doesn't matter—"

I don't let her finish. "Yeah, I know. It doesn't matter because this isn't real." *So, why is it affecting me so much?*

"No. I was going to say it doesn't matter because I don't live according to my dad's expectations. I'm not motivated by money, so whatever he said, let it go," she counters, leaning in the doorway to the bathroom. I'm sure she's thinking of her trust fund. If only she knew I don't give a fuck about that, but I do care about her parents casting her aside like trash.

Rather than respond, I stay silent and finish getting ready. I'm sure she would walk away from them in heartbeat, but I'm not sure it's fair of me to let her.

With nothing left to do but put myself through hell, I walk to Lucy and hold out my arm. "Let's get this night over with, shall we?"

"Let's," she responds, linking her arm through mine as we exit the room for the last supper. Tomorrow can't come soon enough at this rate.

Lucy

Justin didn't say anything while he finished up in the bathroom. I'm not sure what that means. Obviously, something is bothering him from the conversation with my dad earlier, but it doesn't look like anything I say is helping. Once we get back to San Diego tomorrow, and away from all this toxicity, I'm sure he'll forget whatever seems to be eating at him. We just need to make it through tonight.

I was close to Richard's parents all those years ago. Patty and Clint were like a second set of parents after spending so much time at their house. I'm hoping they just want to catch up and have no ulterior motive, such as hoping Richard and I reconnect. Especially since he must have told them I was engaged after running into Justin and me.

We're about to find out when the doorbell chimes to announce their arrival as soon as we descend the stairs. We quickly join my parents in the salon, where we'll start the night over cocktails. Probably a good idea so Justin can loosen up and shake off whatever it is that's causing him distress.

Minutes later, Darryl leads them in. "Lucy, sweetheart, it's so wonderful to see you. Wow, you look so grown up. I can't believe it." Mrs. Siemen is the first to greet me with a hug, Clint and Richard trailing behind.

"Thank you, Patty. It's good to see you, too. It's been so long," I say as we embrace.

"Too long. Isn't that right, Clint?" she asks Richard's dad as we separate.

"Absolutely. We were telling Richard how much we miss the days when you two were inseparable. We enjoyed having you around." Clint reaches for me with outstretched arms.

"You're so sweet, thank you." With both greetings out of the way, I reach for Justin's hand and tug him closer. "Let me introduce you to Justin, my fiancé. Justin, this is Clint and Patty Siemen."

The evening progresses surprisingly well. It's nice catching up with Richard's family and makes me regret my initial reluctance. Justin seems to be handling it well and even enjoying himself.

It's mid-meal when things take a turn for the worse. I should've known this was too good to be true.

"Tell us about your firm, Richard. It sounds like you recently made partner. That's quite an accomplishment at such an early stage in your career," Dad says during a break in conversation as we're all preoccupied with eating.

Richard looks up from his plate, nodding while swallowing his bite, and tells us the details. His firm has fifteen lawyers, six of whom are partners. Then he gets to the good part.

"Interestingly enough, we've been discussing opening a branch in San Diego. They're considering me for the development of a new office there. Not having a family or significant other tying me down makes me a likely candidate."

"That's wonderful, Richard. I'm sure it has more to do with your accomplishments, but congratulations regardless. It sounds like a great opportunity. You know, Lucy works for Sebastian Dubree. Maybe she can make an introduction and get your foot in the door with a large client there," Dad suggests out of turn.

"Dad, our in-house legal team handles everything for Dubree Enterprises. It would be a waste of Richard's time."

"Nonsense. Things are often needed outside of our capabilities, and multiple relationships are always wise to have. Speaking of, you and Richard would make a fine team if he needs help getting their firm up and running there. You were good together back in the day. There's no reason you couldn't be again. Don't you agree, Richard?" Dad addresses him before taking a sip of wine.

My jaw drops at his blatant insinuation with Justin sitting right next to me, whose face hardens at the comment. What is my dad's deal? I liked it better when he ignored my existence. Maybe the engagement ruse was not the perfect solution after all.

Richard looks slightly taken aback before quickly schooling his features. "It did cross my mind when I heard Lucy lived there.

I'll have to reach out while I'm in town to see if there might be any possibilities."

Patty—who is utterly oblivious to the implications of their comments—adds her own. "Oh, that would be so lovely if you were working together. We'd have a part of Lucy back in our lives."

Okay, enough is enough. I need to end this crazy rabbit hole of a conversation. "I'll see what I can do about an introduction, but I'm not looking to leave my job. My current position is perfect, and I've made good friends at work. I'm happy where I am." With that last statement, I squeeze Justin's thigh.

The night continues downhill from there. While I enjoyed reminiscing with Richard and his parents, it didn't feel right to do it with Justin there. My conflicted feelings make it hard to remember that we're not truly a couple. After tonight, who knows what will happen? Justin and I seemed to reconnect, but there was no definitive plan for when we return home. Now I'm not sure what to think, especially with how this whole day has gone.

Thinking clarity would come when we were alone in our room tonight was futile. Justin remained silent while getting ready for bed and muttered a quick good night before turning the light out and sticking to his side of the bed. I'm trying to be understanding and give him space to process whatever is bothering him, hoping we'll talk about it on the way home tomorrow.

In mere days, he went from agreeing to a friends-with-benefits arrangement while working toward a relationship, to giving me the silent treatment. The sad thing is, I'm positive it wouldn't have taken long to reach relationship status, and now I may have lost my chance.

12

FEELING FROSTY

Justin

WHAT A FUCKING SHIT SHOW OF A NIGHT. THAT'S THE first thought that pops into my mind when I wake up on the final morning of the sentence I'm serving in hell. All I know after last night is that if I were Lucy's real fiancé, we would've been out of there halfway through the meal, never looking back.

Since I'm not, all it did was force me to reevaluate the situation and my intentions. The differences between Richard and me are like night and day. He's posh; I'm simple. He's privileged; I'm not. He comes from wealth; I made my own. He's everything Lucy's dad expects for her; I'm the farthest thing from it.

While none of that shit would normally matter to me, there's more on the line than just my pride. It's Lucy's family. And whether she realizes it or not, it's a big deal. I'm not selfish enough to put my wants over Lucy's ultimate happiness. She may not need them now, but someday, she'll see the bigger picture and how a relationship with her mom and dad affects more than just her. Until then, I'll be strong enough to see it for her.

Knowing what's to come, I can't resist holding her one last time. Careful not to wake her, I slowly slide over and gently curl my arm around her while she sleeps. The feel of her warm body up against mine is almost enough to weaken my resolve and throw my steadfast decision out the window. But rather than dwell on it, I cherish the moment and tell myself it'll be all right.

Knowing the alarm is set to go off soon, I breathe her in one last time and memorize the feel of her before pulling back and heading for the shower. The best thing to do is move on and put this week behind me. Forget it ever happened and dive back into work. It's what saved me last time, and it'll have to do the job again.

I'm doing a final rinse when her soft voice drifts over from the doorway. "Mind if I join you?"

The war in my mind is fierce, not to mention the argument from down below, but my resolve wins out. "Come on in. It's all yours. I just finished up."

I step out and quickly grab my towel to wrap around my waist. The less temptation either of us has, the better. If I allow a last hurrah, I might cave—fuck the consequences.

"Oh, okay. Thanks." She's not dumb. It's obvious I've been distant since the discussion with her dad. Yeah, I let my guard down for a bit in the pool yesterday, but other than that, I've kept things casual. It'll make it easier in the long run.

We get ready to go, dancing around each other as we pack up and prepare to leave. She's given up trying to converse, probably as frustrated with me as I am with the entire situation. It's evident we're both on edge when we leave the room with our bags in hand.

We make it to the breakfast room where her parents are waiting to say goodbye. I'm sure they're more than ready to see us off and praying I'm not in the picture by this time next year.

"Good morning. Are you both all set to catch your flight?" her mom asks as we join them at the table.

"We are. We'll grab a quick bite and cup of coffee before we head out," Lucy responds as she fills a plate.

If there's one thing I'll surely miss, it's the food—top-notch and ready whenever you want. Their in-house chef is impressive. I'll at least give them credit for that, and if I ever get to the point where I want to hire frivolous help, that's where I'll start.

"Mr. and Mrs. Alcott, thank you for your hospitality this week. I've enjoyed getting to know you both. And compliments to your chef—the food was delicious." I give my farewell statement, determined to finish this as positively as possible for Lucy's sake.

Her dad, on the other hand, has different ideas. "Likewise. I'm glad we were able to meet and took time to talk so we could be on the same page before you leave. It's best when two people see eye to eye," he says smugly before moving on to his paper.

Lucy gives me the side eye, clearly curious what his cryptic words means, but I receive the message loud and clear.

"I couldn't agree more." *Now get me the fuck out of here.*

Lucy

What the hell is going on? Justin has been downright frosty since yesterday morning, and I'm feeling more irritated by the minute. I've been patient, letting him muddle through his thoughts alone, but my patience has hit its limit. We have twenty minutes left of the last flight into San Diego, and it's time to intervene before it's too late. I'm worried if I let this go on too long, we won't recover from whatever dark place he's in.

"Justin, seriously, I know the talk with my dad has something to do with your one-eighty over the last twenty-four hours. Tell me what he said so I can fix it."

He puts his magazine down and looks at me, the gears in his head clearly turning while contemplating his answer. "The last day was eye-opening." He pauses, sighing. "When we pulled up to your family's estate, it was clear we come from two different worlds. Why I thought that wouldn't be a problem is a mystery to me. But after speaking with your dad and having dinner with your ex's family, I could tell our differences are too big to ignore."

"What are you talking about? I'm still me… Lucy, the executive assistant you met at Dubree Enterprises. Just because my family has money doesn't change anything. I'm no different than I was three days ago."

"You're right, but our backgrounds will cause issues in the future. If we were to end up together, our ideals would be so far from each other that we'd constantly be fighting. It just won't work between us, and it's better to figure that out now than get more involved only to regret it in the end. I should've realized that before I started things up again. I'm sorry."

"You're sorry? Are you kidding me right now? What—you're suddenly a psychic and can see the future? Just like that, you've decided we can't be together because I come from money. Money that isn't mine, that I choose to live without, and have no qualms not getting a dime of. You're backtracking based on some big assumptions."

"I prefer to call it intuition—maybe instinct. You could even go so far as sensible. You may be saying those things now, but this affects your children. You might want to send them to the most expensive schools in the country one day. Look, Lucy, I don't want to string you along just because we're compatible in the bedroom. You deserve someone who will make you happy in the long run, and you'll have plenty of time to find that before going home next year." He gives me a small smile that I want to punch right off his face.

Taking the ring off my finger, I hold it out and drop it into his open palm. "Well then, I guess a thank-you is in order. Thank you for being a coward and for reminding me exactly why I can't trust you."

"Something's not adding up. Are you sure your dad didn't threaten him or something?" Lily asks when I tell her how the week went and how things ended between Justin and me.

"My dad's a jerk, so I wouldn't put it past him, but there's nothing to threaten him with. It simply is what it is. I can't make him want to be with me. And why would I want to be with someone who keeps changing his mind, anyway? This is exactly what he did before. Shouldn't I be grateful he told me to my face this time?"

"Speaking of, I heard some gossip you might be interested in." She wiggles her brows, trying to bait me.

It works. "What did you hear and from who, so I know if it's legit."

"Sebastian and Eli, who know Justin fairly well since they've used his company so much throughout the years. So, did you know he's the one who was first assigned to me before I even knew Sebastian had me being watched?" she asks, making me wince.

"I did, sorry." At the time, I didn't feel guilty because I was happy to have Justin visiting the office to deliver reports, plus I didn't know Lily all that well. Once we became friends, the guilt set in that she was in the dark.

"Don't be. It's just Sebastian's way of caring. But anyway, that's not the point. Apparently, Justin was pretty upset over my kidnapping that night and insisted it was entirely his fault. He took all the blame, removing himself from my protection and assigning replacements. Wasn't that around the time you two were seeing each other?"

"Yeah. But how did this come up while I was gone?"

"Okay, don't get mad, but I told the guys why he went home with you for Christmas since Sebastian already knew a little about it from that day. Then—"

I cut her off. "By the way, I never did give you shit for that. You know he's been trying to promote me ever since? Next time you better warn me when he's around."

She shakes her head in exasperation. "You're crazy, and we're coming back to that, but first, you're missing the point. Why do you think he ended up ghosting you in the first place? Think back to when it happened. Wasn't he with you the night of the kidnapping?" She lets her question hang while I mull that over.

When he left so abruptly the next morning, it was obviously from the phone call about it. At the time, I remember using the whole thing as an excuse when Eli told me what happened. But what if there was more to it?

Lily's looking at me expectantly, so I finally answer her question. "We went to a late dinner that night because he worked the gala. It was the first time he stayed over."

"See? He was with you while something happened to me that he felt responsible for. Maybe that's why he cut things off."

"Maybe, but that still doesn't excuse *how* he did it. And why couldn't he say that? Even last week, he had plenty of time to explain, but he didn't. No, I'm not buying it. And honestly, I'm done looking for excuses."

"I can't blame you there. It just sucks. You guys seem to have this connection, like you're meant to be together or something."

I roll my eyes. "Okay, Miss *I Read Too Many Romance Novels*."

"Oh, whatever. Sue me for wanting you to get your happily ever after."

"I'm not thinking that's in my future quite yet. Burn me once, shame on you. Burn me twice, shame on me."

"You never know… third time's a charm," she says, making me giggle.

"We won't ever know because he's not getting another chance."

"Fine. Maybe we'll find you a new man on New Year's Eve. The party we're going to this weekend will be amazing." She holds her hand up, palm facing me, as my mouth starts to open. "Before you protest, we already bought the tickets, so you're going. You get a plus-one, too, because… well, I thought you guys might be together when you got back—sorry." She looks down in guilt but then pops her head back up. "You could see if Jordan wants to go?"

"I am *not* asking him out. Anyway, I have someone in mind already. My ex, Richard, I told you about? He'll be in town next week for work and asked if I wanted to meet for a drink. I may as well see if he wants to go."

"You're playing with fire, Lucy."

"I've already been burned by Mr. Burns. How much worse can it get?"

13

SECRET SANTA

Justin

HAVEN'T BEEN ABLE TO GET LUCY OUT OF MY HEAD SINCE WE got back, and I've realized she's a distraction whether I'm with her or not. She's taken up permanent residence in my head. After finally deciding not to let my fear of distraction get in the way, her dad's threat put a wrench in my plans. Now, I'm as frustrated as ever, knowing what I want isn't attainable.

My intercom buzzes as I'm wrapping up for the day. "Justin, a Trevor Alcott is on the line. He says he knows you." Why the hell is Lucy's brother calling me? *Fuck, is Lucy okay?*

"Thank you, Macy, I'll take it," I respond, quickly hitting the button to take the call.

"Trevor?"

"Hey, asshole. You remember I warned you about hurting Lucy

again, right?" he says, easing my fear that something happened to Lucy. The only thing to happen to her was me.

"Yeah, I remember."

"What the fuck is your problem? You spend one week with my sister and fuck her over again? Do you get your kicks from playing women, or is it just my sister you enjoy screwing with?" Yep, he's pissed. Once more, it proves how close these two are if she's told him about what happened.

"The last thing I wanted to do was hurt Lucy. There's more to it than that." I'm not sure how close he is to his dad, but telling him what happened might not be the brightest idea.

"Start talking then because I'll get creative to take you down if I have to."

"I'm glad she has you watching out for her, but I think this is between me and Lucy."

"It would be if I hadn't just spent the last half hour on the phone hearing about your bullshit. What the hell, man? It sure seemed like more than just a show. To me, it looked like you were interested in the real deal. Are you really that good, and the whole thing was just an act?"

"It wasn't. If nothing stood in our way, I'd make Lucy part of my future tomorrow. But there are consequences that Lucy doesn't understand. And maybe she thinks she does, but she shouldn't have to choose between me and her family. Whether you realize it or not, my decision was for her own good."

"You mean because of the trust fund or because she won't be welcomed back?"

"Wait—you know?"

Trevor scoffs. "My dad tells me everything, which is how I know you made the wrong decision. Lucy said she told you she didn't care about the money. And did you miss the fact that she already tried to get as far away as possible from our parents in the first place?"

"That's not something she can decide right now. It doesn't only affect her life; it affects her children as well. Lucy doesn't know how she'll feel when her kids have no grandparents. I can't do that to her." The thought of her having a family with some other guy irritates me.

He chuckles. "Funny. She did go off about you being some sort of psychic."

The memory makes me laugh. "Look. This decision didn't come lightly. I don't want to be responsible for messing up her life. I'm not worth it, trust me."

"Too late buddy. And I don't think that's up to you. Maybe you should try talking to her. Fuck… encouragement is the last thing I want to give you because, frankly, I don't even like you, but my sister—she's fucking miserable. Make it right, man. You screwed up. It's obvious there's something between you guys, and if I were you, I wouldn't let my dad ruin that. He's a prick. Why do you think my sister wants nothing to do with our family?"

"That doesn't make me the right choice. It would be easier for her in the long run if she ended up with someone your dad approved of… like Richard."

"Are you fucking serious right now? He's a douchebag. You know they broke up because he cheated on her?"

I drop my head and shake it, letting out a heavy sigh. "No, I didn't." I pause, both of us remaining silent for a beat. "What's done is done, man. I'm not sure what you expect from me."

"For starters, she appears to really like you, and from what I could see, it's reciprocated. The bottom line is—no matter what, tell her the truth and quit making her feel like shit every time you run off. Basically, fix this."

My hackles go up. "And if I don't?"

"Then I'll fix you."

"Why are you here if you're putting me in charge?" Sam asks after I brief him on his New Year's Eve assignment while we stand near the venue's entrance. The two-person team shadowing the Dubrees are inside, already at their posts.

There was no hesitation from me when Mr. Dubree asked for extra security at the New Year's Eve party they were attending. Having received all the details in advance, I knew Lucy would be with them. He didn't blink an eye when I told him I'd provide two people for tonight, one of whom was myself. He still doesn't feel comfortable bringing Lily to large events, which happens to work in my favor.

Rather than serving as active security, though, I'll be focused on Lucy. I need to determine once and for all what I'm going to do about the situation and my inability to stop thinking about her.

"There's something else needing my attention tonight. I'll be on-site but not active."

"Does this have anything to do with the girl you stole from Tom?" He raises his eyebrows in question.

"Stole? Are you fucking kidding me? What are you guys, a bunch of gossips? For the record, I did not steal anyone from Tom. Lucy was never his to begin with. She was always mine."

His hands go up in defense. "Whoa there, boss. I was just asking since that's what I'd heard. No offense."

I decide to ignore his response. "Keep your head in the game and pretend I'm not here. While it'll look like I'm part of the detail, our team will know I'm not. Don't let your eyes drift from your assignment."

"Got it. Good luck with whatever it is you're here for."

"Thanks. Looks like they're pulling up now, so you can take it from here." With that, I slink back toward the building, out of sight, to observe as I contemplate my next move.

Although my team knows I'm not officially on duty tonight, the Dubrees do not, and I don't want them feeling less than protected out of the gate. If the situation changes later—which part of me hopes it will—I'll explain how tonight's security is set up. I say a *part of me* because I've yet to decide which direction I'm taking. The consequences of Lucy being with me are at the forefront of my mind, and I'm still questioning which path to take.

I watch as the valet opens the car door to see Sebastian and Lily exit first, followed by Eli and his date, then Lucy. What I'm not expecting is the last person to appear… *What the fuck?* It's been a week, and already Richard is swooping in to steal the prize.

Lucy

"What's going on, Lucy? He seems perfect. High school sweethearts, estranged for eight years until fate brings you back together. It sounds so romantic, so why does it feel like I'm missing something here?" Lily asks when we slip into the bathroom while the guys refresh our drinks. Eli and his date have gone MIA, to the surprise of no one.

"It does sound perfect, and honestly, I'm not sure. It just doesn't feel right." I shake my head, knowing exactly why it doesn't feel right.

"Dammit, Justin's the problem. I'm pissed that I'm still letting him get to me after being ditched yet again. What's it going to take?" I have serious issues if this last time didn't cure me from being hung up on him.

"The problem is you've got it bad. But the thing is, Richard's here now, so maybe you should try to enjoy the moment and see where it takes you."

"Yeah, you're right. Okay, I'm gonna shake this off. Luckily, it's easy with Richard since we have so much history."

"Speaking of, why did you guys break up anyway?" Lucy asks.

"At senior prom, I caught him kissing another girl. He said it was because he was too drunk, and she cornered him, but whatever. I was leaving for college, so I didn't care. We weren't meant to last."

"Oh wow, that sucks."

"Exactly, which is why it's not going anywhere. He was just the easy button for tonight. That doesn't mean I shouldn't pull my head out of my ass and start having fun, though. Thanks for the talk."

"Of course. That's what friends are for. Let's go see if the guys got our drinks." She throws her arm around me, and we exit the bathroom to find both of them waiting outside the door.

It's no surprise that Sebastian is antsy. He doesn't let Lily out of his sight in public places for long—poor guy. I don't think he'll ever recover from her kidnapping. I'm surprised she does so well with it, although I do notice she's very protective of her drinks, which was how it happened in the first place.

Sebastian folds Lily into his arms as if he'd been waiting a week to hold her. It's sweet. Meanwhile, Richard smiles from a few feet away and holds my drink out when I join him.

"Hey," he says as I take it.

"Hey. Thanks for the drink. Sorry if we took too long."

"You didn't. Sebastian doesn't do lines, so we were fast. Man, he's an intense guy, isn't he?"

I laugh, being quite familiar with his intensity. "That's one way to put it. Did you guys end up talking at all, or was he preoccupied with waiting for Lily?"

"I'm going to go with the latter unless telling me 'we should get the ladies' is considered conversation."

"With Sebastian, you might want to take it. He's not very articulate unless it's about work, Lily, his brother, or in conversation with one of those two. So, don't take it personally."

"Good to know. Maybe you should consider coming on board with our firm. I'm way more fun than that guy." He raises a brow, making me laugh again.

We have such easy banter. I think I'm ready to relax and be in the moment like Lily suggested. It's time to let loose and see where the night goes.

14

MAKE MY WISH COME TRUE

Justin

'M NO CLOSER TO CHOOSING WHAT TO DO NOW THAN THE beginning of the night. I've been staying in the shadows, watching, trying to decide, but the more I see, the more it appears she's doing just fine without me. Richard seems to have no problem making her laugh, that's for sure. Who knows, maybe he was simply young and made an immature mistake.

Seeing her laugh at that dick again makes me want to hurt someone, and since the only thing I've accomplished tonight is feeling like a stalker, I decide it's time to bow out gracefully. There's nothing here for me, and the Dubrees have plenty of security in place with their two bodyguards and my number one on-site.

I'll make sure Sam knows I'm heading out and then drown my New Year's sorrows alone. The last time I saw him, he was following

Sebastian and Lily out of the room. Those two taking off is a common occurrence from the stories I hear.

I'm still searching twenty minutes later. It feels like I've been all over this place without catching sight of anyone when I round the corner and stop short at the scene near the end of the hallway. Richard is there with Lucy, backed up against the wall in a passionate embrace. Fucking great—that's the last thing I need seared into my brain. But as I turn to backtrack, something catches my eye. The woman's hair isn't blonde. *What the fuck?*

When I'm close enough, I take it upon myself to interrupt. "Hey, man, seems like you're having a good time tonight."

Richard leaps back at the sound of my voice, guilty as hell. The woman takes one look at my face and hurries off, leaving the two of us alone.

"Justin. Hey. I didn't know you were here tonight. Lucy said you guys had called things off."

"What's your deal, man? You figure sampling the goods is the best way to get back into Lucy's good graces? Just like old times, huh?"

"Sometimes shit happens. Lucy's great, but we don't have that spark like we used to." This man-to-man talk isn't cutting it with me.

"Does she know that, or were you planning on double-dipping? What she doesn't know won't hurt her?" My anger is rising, and keeping my temper in check is difficult.

"Come on, man. Lucy and I are just getting reacquainted. Who knows what'll happen between us?" His shoulders shrug as if it's no big deal.

"I do, so let me fill you in. You're going to go in there, say goodbye, and tell Lucy you're not mature enough for a relationship. Or I can take care of it for you. What's it going to be?"

"I'll say goodbye. I didn't mean any harm. Sorry, man." Richard raises his arms, palms out in defense.

My head jerks in the direction of the main room. "I'm not the one you should be apologizing to. Hurry up before I change my mind and decide to handle this with my fists."

Lucy

This New Year's officially sucks. Eli and his date took off earlier, Sebastian and Lily disappeared thirty minutes ago, and Richard still hasn't returned from the bathroom. I'm trying to stay positive… Oh, who am I kidding? I am not at all positive. If this is any indication of how my year will go, I may as well tuck my tail between my legs and sneak out.

The waitress arrives with my drink, their specialty: a raspberry gimlet with a fired orange on top. She hands it to me, the orange still flaming. I figure *what the hell*, and close my eyes, before opening them and blowing out the orange. It'll take a miracle to make my wish come true. Bottoms up to that.

"Lucy, sorry I was gone so long." I'm interrupted with half of my drink left.

Lowering my head and moving my glass down, I see a guilty-looking Richard.

Lifting my gimlet in a mock toast, I respond, "No worries, I had company." I nod towards the drink and smile.

He cringes remorsefully. "Hey, so, I think I'm gonna take off. Thank you for bringing me tonight and introducing me to Sebastian, but I think I'm going to call it a night." He glances at something over my shoulder and continues, "I don't think I'm ready for a relationship, and you deserve more than what I can give you. I'm sorry, Lucy."

What. The. Hell? My eyes narrow when I notice remnants of lipstick around his mouth. How do I continue setting myself up for disappointment? Once a cheater, always a cheater. I should have known better. "Sure. I'm glad you realized that now instead of later. No sense wasting our time." I can't help my snarky tone, or how familiar that sounded.

He leans in for a hug that I reluctantly reciprocate. "Happy New Year, Lucy. And for what it's worth, I hope you find your happy ending. You shouldn't give up on Justin just yet." *What the actual?*

"Uh, where did that come from?" I ask as we pull away.

"It's just a feeling. Anyway, enjoy the rest of your night. I'll see you around."

He walks off as I stand there dumbfounded. I'm so unbelievably lost right now. What did I do to deserve this shit luck? I seem to be in the habit of repelling men at this point.

Since I haven't been watching the time, I'm surprised when the DJ announces to find a partner for the final countdown to the New Year. Great. I lift my drink in salute, figuring that since I was interrupted last time, there's no time like the present to drown my sorrows. The crowd begins to shout.

Ten…

Nine…

Eight…

Seven…

Six…

Five…

Four…

Three…

Two…

My drink is suddenly lifted from my hands.

One…

I'm engulfed in two large, strong arms.

"Happy New Year, Lucy." And then I'm kissed—kissed as if the man is dying of starvation, and my lips are the only sustenance that will save him. I'm completely and utterly ravaged.

His lips move down my jaw and neck to nip my ear. "I'm so sorry, baby. You were right. I was a coward, an ass, an idiot, and everything in between. But most of all, I was scared." His mouth returns to mine, kissing me again before moving to my other ear. "I've decided I'd rather be scared with you than miserable without you. I didn't realize how empty life was until you came along. I've been a shell of a man. And Lucy…?" He looks at me intensely. "With you, I'm whole."

My mind is a jumbled mess. Between his kisses and words, I'm practically incoherent. "Justin… how… when did you get here?"

"I've been here all night, watching you, waiting for a sign to tell me the right thing to do, and it came. You're meant for me, and I'm meant for you, fuck all the consequences. I'll grovel as much as it takes for one last chance." He places his hands on my face, his pleading eyes boring into mine. "Please say yes to coming home with me so I can tell you how wrong I was and show you how right we are together."

"Yes," I reply simply, and all I can think is… my wish came true.

Justin

Lucy must've been too shell-shocked on the way here to say anything because the entire ride was silent, which is fine by me since there was less chance for her to change her mind before we arrived. I'm unlocking the front door quicker than ever, anxious to get her inside. The need to have Lucy in my space consumes me. Once she's within my four walls, she'll be mine. Irrational, I know, but my mind likes to play tricks on me.

Shutting the door, I take her coat and hang it on the coat rack.

"Come on, we can sit in the living room with the fire. Would you like water or wine? I have your favorite white." I stopped at the store earlier today to get everything Lucy liked. You could say I was hopeful.

"As much as I'd like the wine, I better stick with water for now," she says as she sits on the couch.

"Be right back." I flick the switch for the fire before heading towards the kitchen. Just before turning the corner, I stop and look back. "Lucy, thank you for coming. I'm glad you're here." Then I continue, not giving her the chance to respond.

After putting two glasses of water on the table and sitting beside her, I take the opportunity to start things off. "Even though I'm dying to have you in my arms again, you deserve to have your questions answered and lay into me all you want for how I ended things… again. I'll give you as much time as you need—or until my willpower snaps, whichever comes first. And I make no guarantees how long that will take, so you better get going."

She takes a deep breath and dives right in. "What happened to our different backgrounds being a problem for you? And I thought my *ideals* were too far off from yours. What changed your mind?"

I release my breath slowly, considering the best way to answer. Honesty is usually the best policy, but I don't want to throw her dad under the bus simply for my benefit at the risk of making her feel bad. Instead, I start by explaining my behavior from the first time around, all while deliberating what to say about the more re-cent events.

When I finish explaining where my mind was at after Lily's kidnapping, she doesn't hesitate to chime in. "Why didn't you tell me this right away, or even last week? What if something bad hap-pens at work again, and you end up in a similar situation? I don't want to be constantly looking over my shoulder, waiting for you to disappear." Her response is warranted.

I can't resist reaching for her hand. "That's fair. To answer your question, I didn't say anything last week because I wanted you to take me back with no excuses. If you gave me a second chance after handling things so poorly, I wanted it to be of your own free will. Look… what both situations boil down to is communication and feelings. I'm not great with either. From the military to owning a security firm, my world has always been black and white."

"So, how will you be in a relationship that might add some color to your world?"

"The company I've built thrives on my leadership, organiza-tion, and training. The action was fun for a while, but trust me baby, you're more fun, I promise. I'll still take the occasional small job or low-security gig, but I'll assign my team the rest. That's what they're trained for, and I'll focus more on the business end of things."

"And my family? Our different upbringings? You insisted that was a deal-breaker a few days ago. That seems pretty black and white to me. What changed?" She's not making this easy.

"There are differences between us, but they don't matter to me. I only said those things because you shouldn't have to choose between me and your family, so I chose for you. I had good inten-tions but went about it the wrong way again. My good intentions were thrown out the window after enduring this past week without you. I realize your choices shouldn't be made for you, but it's important you understand what you'd be giving up." This is the part I'm absolutely dreading.

"My dad told you, didn't he? About my trust fund?" She looks down, shaking her head and pulls her hand from mine. "So that's why they didn't sound surprised when I told them we broke up. Did you not believe me when I said I don't want it?"

I grab her hand again. "Lucy, there's more to it than that. I don't want you to have any regrets."

"So it's okay to regret losing you but not my trust fund?"

"It's not just your trust fund you'd be losing, sweetheart." I bring her hand up and softly kiss it. "Your dad made it clear that if we married, they would no longer be a part of your life. I'm not worth a future with no parents."

"That's for me to decide. What if you are my future?" Her baby-blue eyes stare at me, full of emotion.

I look up at the ceiling and exhale loudly. "Christ, you have no idea how badly I want that… but you shouldn't decide tonight. Take some time to think it through. How about this? Let's start over—date. Get to know each other all over again and see where it goes. What do you think?"

"Well… I guess the third time's a charm. But I'm telling you now, if it ends up being a strike, you're out for good this time."

"I'm going for a home run, baby."

"Are you running or walking? Because I'm ready to—"

My lips cut her off. That's enough talking for tonight. I'm sure we have many battles ahead, but for now, I can't think of a better way to start the new year than burying myself deep inside my woman until I'm etched into her soul, the same way she's infiltrated mine.

Epilogue

Lucy

I T'S VALENTINE'S DAY AND JUSTIN'S TAKING ME TO A SWANKY new restaurant downtown. I came home from work to change and get ready for the evening. We've been bouncing back and forth between his house and mine, spending more nights together than not.

Justin's been true to his word, *dating* me since New Year's. But now I'm ready for more. We haven't said the L word yet, and I'm working up the nerve to say it tonight, even if it's not reciprocated. I've felt it for a while but haven't found the right moment to tell him.

At Justin's request, I haven't told my parents we're seeing each other again. He didn't want any interference while building our relationship, and we both know they'd interfere plenty if they found out. He also wanted to avoid causing any unnecessary problems if

I changed my mind. I've assured him that won't happen—that my decision is final, but despite that, he's still insisting I wait.

Since we're staying at his house tonight, I'm tossing clothes into a bag when the doorbell rings. I give myself a once-over in the entryway mirror before opening the door to a delicious looking Justin, smelling good enough to eat.

Maybe we should skip dinner.

"Hey, gorgeous." He comes in, shutting the door behind him and wrapping me in his arms. "Happy Valentine's Day, baby. You should've stayed over last night so I could've told you the second your eyes opened. Plus, I'm getting used to having you in my bed. I missed you." His lips graze mine before kissing their way toward my ear, nipping it with his teeth. "Maybe you should consider letting your lease go."

Hold up—did he just ask me to move in with him? I think he missed a step. I must take too long to find my voice, because he pulls back and carries on like he didn't just drop a bombshell on me.

"Is your bag ready to go? We have reservations at seven, so we should get going."

"Uh… yeah. Let me grab one last thing." I'm still a little blown away by his comment. It could've just been a passing thought, nothing literal. Or… maybe he realized what he said and changed his mind right away. Oh my God, this is going to bug me all night.

He follows me to the bedroom where I grab a nightgown, but he takes it out of my hand before it makes it to the bag.

"You won't need that," he says, throwing it on the bed and zipping the bag.

"Justin," I admonish.

"Yes, dear?" he calls, already halfway to the front door.

I shake my head and follow, grabbing my coat on the way out.

"I took on a new client today. It was a referral from the Dubrees and requires surveillance. The request reminds me of Sebastian and Lily's initial situation."

"Really? How so?" We're sitting in the restaurant, having just finished dinner, waiting for dessert to arrive.

"Well, this Jackson guy wants a girl followed who will have no idea we're protecting her. The difference this time is that we know upfront she's in danger. It makes us more diligent and requires greater focus than cases only requesting tracking."

"I think I know who Jackson is, if it came from the Dubrees. But anyway, that's good, right? Referrals are what business is made of."

"Definitely. But the reason I'm telling you is because it brought back memories of the situation with Lily and how my actions impacted what happened." He's looking at me intently, like his next words are difficult to say.

"Oh." This is it. He's breaking up with me the night I was going to tell him I loved him. On Valentine's Day, for Christ's sake.

The waiter arrives with dessert, giving pause to the conversation. Thank God—it buys time to collect my thoughts and mentally prepare for the final blow.

We each take a bite before talking. Justin hums in approval, while mine is simply tasteless at this point. My stomach is doing somersaults in anticipation of the impending breakup.

Justin finally continues. "Anyway, my initial reaction was to do the job myself… maybe to redeem myself, if you will."

"If you need time apart to focus on work, just tell me. It's okay,

Justin. I'm a big girl." I'll do my best to make it appear that way, anyway.

He shakes his head. "No. What I'm trying to say, and doing a piss-poor job of, is that the only person I need to redeem myself to is you. So, I assigned Sam." He reaches for my hand across the table, holding it as he gazes at me. Meanwhile, my heart thunders in my chest. "I've discovered I like the color you add to my life, and I've decided I want more. I love you, Lucy."

The breath I'd been holding rushes out, and I press a hand to my chest. "Oh my gosh, that is not what I was expecting."

He looks surprised by my words. "Is that a good or bad thing?"

"Good. So good. Justin, I love you, too."

His face lights up. "You have no idea how nice it is to hear those words from your lips." He squeezes my hand.

"Same. It's a relief to finally say it. I've wanted to for a while but was afraid to be the first. I've been trying to work up the courage. I was finally going to tell you tonight."

"How about we take the rest of dessert home, and you can tell me again when we get there. And then again while we're in bed. And again, as I fill you with my cock. Then you can tell me how much you love both of us."

My core clenches as my head nods an enthusiastic yes.

Justin

"Thank you again for the flowers—they're beautiful. I left them at the office so I can look at them all week. I'll bring them home on Friday," Lucy says as we walk in the door, and I take her coat.

"I'm glad. Speaking of home, what did you think of my suggestion earlier?" I raise my eyebrow, trying to downplay my anxiousness for her response. To ease the pressure, I head into the kitchen and open a bottle of wine from the fridge. After pouring two glasses, I hand one to Lucy, seated at the breakfast bar, still not answering the question.

"Well?" I ask, taking a sip.

"I'm assuming you're referring to letting my lease go?"

I nod.

"Are you asking me to move in with you?" she asks shyly.

I nod again.

"Hmm," is all she says before taking an excruciatingly slow sip of wine.

Remaining silent, I raise my eyebrows impatiently.

"Well… are you ready to accept my decision and let me tell my parents we're together?"

"That depends. Are you ready to lose not only your trust fund but the relationship with your mom and dad?"

"That depends. Are you ready to let me?" Her petulant tone surfaces, along with a hint of defiance.

"Did you know I love you?" I ask, trying to soften the moment. Her giggle tells me it worked.

"Say it again." She brings her hands to her mouth in excitement.

"I love you."

"Again?" Fuck, she's adorable with her cute little smile.

"Would you like me to show you how much I love you?" I ask seductively, ready to do just that.

She nods.

I set my wine down, take her hand, and gently pull her off the stool. Then I scoop her into my arms, bridal style, making her squeal.

"Justin, what are you doing?"

"I'm carrying you to our bed, my dear, so I can love you the way you deserve to be loved."

"We haven't decided that it's *our* bed yet."

I pause in the hallway before crossing the threshold to the room and look into Lucy's eyes. "It became *our* bed six weeks ago on New Year's, and it will remain that way, whether you decide to make this your home or not. Now, are you ready to see all the ways I can love you in our bed?"

"More than ready."

"Me too, baby. Trust me." I gently kiss her lips before moving across the room and laying her down, head resting on the pillows.

I brush the hair from her temple and bend down to rest my lips there, breathing in her scent. "Do you trust me enough to give up your control, so I can make your body sing?"

"What do you mean?"

"I want you spread out for me, tied up and blindfolded." I move my lips to her ear and whisper. "Show your trust in me by surrendering your body, and I'll make tonight the most pleasurable night of our lives. Think you can you do that?"

Her panting tells me she's turned on by the idea, but I sense hesitation.

"Say yes, baby. Let me love you."

"Yes," she breathes.

"That's my girl. You won't regret it, Lucy." I rise and give directions before leaving. "Get naked for me while I go grab a few things. I'll be back soon." I start to walk away, but stop, deciding to throw something else out for fun. "Don't think about touching my pussy while I'm gone. Got it?"

She nods in agreement, a little smirk on her face.

Stepping into the closet, I take a few deep breaths. My cock aches in anticipation of what's coming. Fuck, this woman is everything to me. Sex between us is more than I ever thought possible, but this is going to take her pleasure to the next level, and I'm eager to see her reaction. She has no idea what she's in for tonight.

Taking more time than necessary is intentional, dragging it out to build her anxiety—not to mention her desire. Slowly, I gather everything needed, wondering if she's following my orders not to touch herself. Sure enough, as I leave the closet, I catch her hand right above her pussy, hesitating, dying to move those last couple inches.

"Lucy, were you about to touch yourself when I specifically told you not to?"

Her hand jerks back. "No."

"Is your pussy begging for attention, my dear?" I ask as I walk to the bed, setting my supplies on the nightstand.

"Yes."

"Hmm. Let me see if she's weeping enough to get what she wants." My hand reaches her beautiful pussy, and I slowly probe her entrance with my fingers, leisurely stroking in and out. She's fucking drenched.

"Baby, she's so wet for me. You'll have to be patient, while I get you ready. Don't worry, though, she'll get the fucking she's begging for soon enough. Until then—the more tears, the better." I remove my fingers, slick with her juices.

"Please, Justin, I need more." Her hips rock.

I chuckle. "Time to get you tied up, sweetheart. You're not in control tonight, remember?"

"Who are you kidding? I'm never in control."

"Oh, Lucy. If you only knew."

Ten minutes later, she's sufficiently secured. Each limb is

strapped to a bedpost, spreading her out like a star across the mattress. I had her watch as I tied each one, allowing her to see exactly what I was doing so she'd feel comfortable the first time. The blindfold is all that's left, but first, I step back and slowly undress, letting her take in the show. My cock is rock hard, and she's squirming in the restraints, her eyes locked on it. She's a beautiful sight to behold.

"Are you ready to let go, baby? Think you can handle the dark?"

"What if I can't?"

"I won't do anything I don't think you can take. You'll be okay, I promise. And you can tell me to stop anytime if it's too much."

"Then, yes, I'm ready."

"Good girl."

I place the sleeping mask over her eyes, then place a scarf over it, tying it around her head securely to ensure she can't see.

"I'll be back in a minute."

"WHAT? You can't just leave me here. Where are you going?" There's a note of panic in her voice.

"Shhh. It's okay. You're safe." I kiss her lips and circle her gorgeous nipple with my finger, making her moan. She bucks her pelvis as much as she can with her legs stretched wide.

"I think next time, I'll need a strap around the bed to secure your hips," I say, amused.

"Justinnn," she wines as I pull away.

Leaving her whimpering, I head to the kitchen and grab a bowl of ice and glass of wine. When I return to the bedroom, I pause, taking a moment to admire the beauty laid out before me. She's stunning. Her body is a work of art. The fact that she's mine and tied up at my mercy makes me want to say fuck it and sink my cock deep inside her where it belongs. But tonight is for her pleasure as much as mine. We'll both be satisfied by the time I'm through with her.

Lucy

The sound of Justin's footsteps gives away his return, but they stop halfway to the bed. I listen for more, hearing nothing. My core is throbbing, and I feel my wetness dripping onto the sheets beneath me. I don't think I've ever been this turned on in my life, and he hasn't even touched me yet. I'm getting impatient for what's next.

"Justin, what are you doing?" I know he's there.

"Admiring the view, my dear. Do you know how beautiful you are, all splayed out for me and at my mercy? I can see your pussy glistening with tears from here."

"Stop staring and get over here, or I'll be the one crying."

"Fuck, baby, don't tempt me. What I wouldn't do to see you weep for my cock. You're lucky I'm just as worked up, or I might have brought you there."

He moves closer, pausing near the bed. The sound of glass being set on the nightstand is distinct. A few seconds later, his lips graze my nipple, causing me to gasp in surprise. But nothing compares to the hiss I release at the shock of cold when he opens his mouth.

I pull on my restraints as Justin's mouth moves around my breast, letting the ice melt along the way. His hand fondles the other while he concentrates with the ice around my nipple, almost to the point of burning, before sucking it into his mouth and flicking my tight bud with his tongue. I cry out in ecstasy right before he releases it with a pop.

"How are you doing so far? You want more?"

"Yes. More, please," I beg, making him chuckle.

There's a brief silence before a cool liquid lands between my breasts, drops continuing steadily downward. When they reach my clit, I squeal. Fuck. I need him to touch me already. I'm desperate for release at this point.

I hear the glass being set on the table seconds before Justin's tongue begins to lap up the liquid.

"Mmm. You taste so good, baby. Nothing like a little wine to make you even more delicious. I can't wait to drink it from your pussy."

Oh fuck. He's killing me right now. I'm going to die of sexual frustration.

The sound of ice clinking catches my attention, and I figure he'll give my other nipple the same treatment. Instead, my hips jolt from the ice being pressed between my legs, while his lips light me on fire. Oh, for all that's holy.

"Oh my God, Justin. Ahh, please, please. I need it sooo bad."

"Oh, don't worry, baby, you're going to get it."

The ice travels further south, and when it reaches my entrance, he pushes it inside with his tongue, causing me to squirm. Then he licks slowly up to my clit and flicks it before he's gone, leaving me a whimpering mess.

"All right, are you ready to have some fun?"

"Yes, because this isn't," I pout.

"Just for that, I'm not taking it easy on you. Open your mouth, Lucy."

I hesitate, not sure what I'm in for.

"Now." I slowly open. "Good girl. Wider. That's it."

The bed dips beside my head, first one side, then the other.

"Wider, baby," he says from above.

I stretch to my max right before his cock slides into my mouth all the way to my throat, making me gag at the unexpected intrusion. My pussy clenches hard as he pulls out and does it again.

"That's it, choke on me, baby. Need that slickness. Just like that. Fuck, your mouth was made for my cock." Once his length is smeared with saliva, he continues rapidly thrusting in and out.

"Goddamn, I could fuck this mouth all night. You take it so good, Lucy." My need grows as he carries on. Suddenly, he retracts so only the tip remains in my mouth.

"You ready for your turn? Keep sucking me, baby. I won't go deep, so suck hard. Oh yeah, just like that. Fuck yeah, you got it."

I can feel the puddle of liquid on the bed beneath me as my pussy aches to be touched, so when his mouth finally makes contact, I can't stop the scream that escapes.

His hips pause for a moment. "I'm gonna come if you keep screaming around my cock like that, baby. Control yourself, or you'll get a mouth full, just like I'm about to."

With those final words, he strikes, sucking my clit while his tongue circles it. I refrain from screaming again but can't hold back my moans. Then, when his fingers plunge into me, it's impossible not to turn my head to the side for desperately needed air.

"Oh my God. Oh my God. Justin! Yes!"

"I'm thirsty, baby. You gonna come for me? Let me drink my fill?"

I break, falling over the edge, gushing as he replaces his hand with his mouth, lapping up everything I've got. I shout my release, struggling against my bonds until he gives me a reprieve, and I'm able to catch my breath from one of the best orgasms of my life.

Justin

She shudders under me, and I'm so ready to shove my cock inside her that I can't wait a second longer. While she's still in a daze from her orgasm, I take the opportunity to position myself between her bound legs that are spread wide for me and without warning, thrust deep in one go.

She groans as her walls clench around me.

"Fuck, Lucy, your pussy is so tight like this. You feel like heaven."

Seeing her tied up, at my mercy, is the hottest thing in the world. But having her trust, knowing I can do anything I want to her, is the biggest turn-on of all.

I relentlessly drive into her with every ounce of strength, hungry for her sounds.

"Do you love this cock, baby? Tell me. Tell me how much you love it."

"I love your cock, Justin. You feel so good. Don't stop, please."

"I'll go all night for you, but I'm slowing down for a minute."

Needing Lucy to understand just how much this means to me, I remove her blindfold, and look into her eyes, hoping she sees the truth in mine. "I love you, Lucy. Fuck, do I love you."

"Justin, I love you so much," she pants out.

And then I devour her mouth, pouring all my love into the kiss, feeling hers in return. My hips move at a leisurely pace, steadily building both of our climaxes. The angle with her legs flat on the bed feels incredible. Hell, everything with Lucy is incredible.

Propping myself up, I reach down and circle her clit with my thumb. "You have another one for me, baby? I need to feel you squeeze my cock, so I can fill you up. Give me your pleasure, my love. Come for me."

"Justin, yes. Oh, God. Yes, yes, fuck!" She explodes around me, pulling me over the edge with her.

"Fuck, Lucy. Your pussy feels so good. Yeah, baby. Fuck, fuck." Our releases merge, and I collapse, pumping every last drop into her.

"Holy shit, Lucy. Every time I think it can't possibly get any better, it does. Shit, woman, you're it for me, you know that?" I slowly pull out, kissing her gently on the lips, and work quickly to undo each binding. The Velcro releases easily, thank God, because all I want to do is hold her.

I pull down the covers and slide in next to her. We're both sated as I gather her in my arms, rubbing her shoulders to ease the tension after being stretched out for so long.

"You haven't said anything yet. Did I fuck you speechless, baby?"

She looks up at me and smiles. "You did."

"How do you feel about what we just did? You okay?" I ask, needing to be sure, even though she seemed to enjoy it.

"It was incredible. Everything was perfect, and I feel amazing. I agree with you—it does keep getting better."

"Why do hear a 'but' coming?"

She scoots back, prompting me to roll onto my side so we're facing each other.

"Well, I'm hung up on your last comment. How can I be it for you if you won't let me say the same?"

I sigh. "I suppose we should finish this conversation. You understand that choosing me means giving up your inheritance? And not only that, but your parents might never speak to you again. You're willing to lose that relationship?"

"Justin, there's a reason I moved thousands of miles away from them. My parents and I were never close. It's their money, not mine. If I cared about it, I would have stayed in Florida instead of going my own way after college."

"Are you sure, baby? Because I won't give you up again. If you choose me, you're mine for good, for better or worse."

"I'm positive. I choose you. I don't care if you clean toilets for a living… Well, okay, maybe I'd care a tiny bit, but what I mean is, we don't need all the money in the world. I love you for who you are, not for what you have. Wait… you said for better or worse, you don't mean marriage, right?" She pulls back in shock.

"I do have the ring," I say, trying to rile her.

"Uhh…"

"I'm kidding. For now. But I'm not kidding about moving in together. What do you say?"

She smiles, her answer clear even before she speaks. "Well… I guess I'll have to since I won't be getting my big inheritance. I'll need to start saving money, so it's a good thing you asked," she teases.

"Good thing." I grin, grabbing her and tickling her sides.

"Justin!" she squeals, laughing uncontrollably.

I ease up, giving her a chance to catch her breath. "Would now be a good time to mention I'm *almost* as rich as your parents?"

"Wait. What?" Her mouth hangs open in shock.

"I mean I'm not completely sure what your family is worth, but I'm probably not too far behind."

"How? And why are you just now telling me?"

"Because I didn't want it to sway your decision, and I'm not one to flaunt it. It's new money from a few years back. A buddy of mine talked me into investing in crypto early on, and it paid off— big time."

She stares at me like I'm an alien or something.

"Say something," I prompt.

"So, you're telling me you're footing the bill for our kids to go to the most expensive schools in the country then?"

I give her a wicked grin and tickle her again. "As long as you don't insist on naming our daughter Victoria."

She pushes me onto my back and climbs on top. "I think I could change your mind."

"Of that, my dear, I have no doubt. Come here," I demand, pulling her down for round two.

Read on for the first two chapters of *Dangerous Pursuit* the next book in *The Pursuit Series*.

Mia Nightingale Marcos is more nightmare than nightingale.

I'm handed the reins to the family business along with an inexperienced assistant barely out of high school. Not to mention, she's distractingly beautiful and completely off-limits. I plan to be so unbearable she'll quit, but she's tougher than she looks. Now she appears to be hiding something and the deeper I dig, the more invested I become, causing my world to spin.

Just when I think I've got her figured out, she vanishes, leaving a trail of unanswered questions, sending me on a dangerous pursuit.

Jackson Soloman is the boss from hell.

But I can handle him. Balancing work by day and poker by night was a breeze until Jackson stepped in. It was easier when he was making my life hell, not trying to play hero. Now, I can't shake him off, and with the growing attraction between us, I'm not sure I want to.

Just when I think I've hit the jackpot, I'm forced to fold, leaving everything behind for a chance at salvation.

Will Mia and Jackson survive the trials of deceit and danger that lie ahead? In a heart-wrenching climax that tests their love and commitment, every decision could be their last bet.

1

NEW BEGINNINGS

Jackson

"Y OU HAVE GOT TO BE KIDDING ME." I'M STARING AT MY parents with my mouth open in shock.

"Jackson, Sofia's had a hard life, and if we can do something as simple as give her daughter a job to show some kindness, then that's what we're going to do. Her husband walked out on her and that poor girl five years ago. He just left them to gamble his life away." My mom has always had a bleeding heart.

"Mom, she's seventeen, for fuck's sake. She's barely out of diapers, and you expect her to be my assistant? Do you know what that entails?" I'm outraged. And that's putting it mildly. I knew Cindy, my executive assistant, was going on maternity leave soon, but I'd already talked to her about hiring someone from a temp agency to take her place until she returned. Instead, they want a high schooler to do her job.

Not only have I been managing the company alone since my sister, Cici, decided she wanted no part of the family business, but now I'm being forced to do it with an immature, inexperienced teenager. It's hard enough without the partner I thought I'd have with my sister. If it weren't for Cindy, my overly competent assistant, I might have run away like Cici.

As it is, my goal is to take us beyond anything they ever hoped for, which I've been doing a damn good job of so far. This, however, could be a significant setback. Since my parent's retirement, my focus has been on growth, having several deals in the works for sales and acquisitions of multiple properties, and now they're asking me to navigate it with inadequate help.

"I do know what it entails, Jackson. I stepped down a year ago, not long enough to forget. I'm also aware that Mia is a bright young lady who will do just fine after being trained by Cindy. You're overreacting. Young people are eager and make excellent employees. Don't be so dramatic." Mom is running the show on this one, while Dad has been uncharacteristically quiet, obviously making this her decision.

"Since you've already committed, it is what it is. But just so we're clear, I *will* make other arrangements if she can't keep up. I'm knee-deep in contract negotiations right now, and I need someone on top of their game. If she's not up to the task, I'll have to find someone who is." My mom can put her foot down on hiring her since this is still technically their company, but if I set my expectations up front, I'll have more firing power later.

My dad finally speaks up. "I agree, son. Give her a chance, and if she doesn't work out, we'll reevaluate the situation and find a different position for her."

"All right, one chance. When should I have Cindy start

training her? She's still six weeks out, so a month from now?" Having my dad's back makes me more agreeable.

"I already made the arrangements, dear," Mom cuts in. "She starts on Monday. Even though Cindy's not due for another month and a half, she could go into labor before then. This way, Mia will be fully trained in case."

Fuck. My. Life.

I dial Braden as soon as I pull out of the driveway. "I need a drink. Meet me at the club?"

"Yeah, sure. What's got you so riled up?"

"Just leaving my parents'. I'll fill you in when I get there. See you soon." If anyone can talk me down, he can.

I don't have to tell him what club we're headed to. Ever since I helped our friend Eli with a business transaction he was doing, we've been on the VIP list at a local nightclub he owns. It's a nice perk: good service, prime tables, and plenty of hot women.

Braden is waiting on the sidewalk when I arrive. "Hey. What went down with your parents to put you in such a mood?"

"Fuck. This takes the cake, man. They have me running the company yet are insisting I replace Cindy with a fucking seventeen-year-old high schooler while she's on maternity leave. I'm livid." I run my hand through my hair and sigh in frustration. I'm so pissed I can't see straight.

"Dude, you can't even bang her. That sucks."

I laugh along with him. Leave it to Braden to lighten the mood. "You got that right. Come on, let's go find someone I can."

Mia

Glancing at the clock on the computer screen, I realize it's time to call it. Shoot. I'm on a winning streak, but oh well. Mom will be home soon, and I'd be in big trouble if she caught me playing online poker. I've made it this far with my secret; I'm not screwing up now.

If she knew this was what I did in my spare time, she'd probably take away all electronics, cancel Wi-Fi, and anything else she could think of to stop me. All thanks to my dad, who walked out five years ago because of his addiction, which just so happens to be gambling in the form of poker. The good news? He taught me everything he knew. I've played since I was old enough to count and surpassed my dad's talent at an early age. Being a whiz with numbers is handy, but my real strength is hiding emotions, which is crucial when playing live games.

When I saw how hard my mom was working to support us after he left, I decided to help. She thinks we get the extra money from a part-time job I made up. She'd keel over from shame if she found out the truth. I don't think she's recovered from my dad leaving us, even after all these years.

After an hour in the kitchen, I hear the front door close seconds before she walks in. "Ooh, what did you make tonight, honey? It smells delicious."

"Some pollo guisado tonight. It's almost finished. I figured you could take the leftovers to work with you tomorrow."

"Oh, mija, you're so good to me. I'll set the table. I have something exciting to tell you over dinner." She looks ecstatic, piquing my curiosity.

We dig in as soon as our butts hit the chairs. Cooking is something I picked up over the last few years. With the internet to provide recipes, I could probably make anything out there, and if groceries weren't so expensive, I'd be able to prove that theory.

"So, what's the exciting news?" I figured she'd get right to it, but we've been silent for the first five minutes, devouring our meals.

"Have I ever mentioned Jack and Hazel Soloman, the nice couple I clean for on Fridays? They were one of my first clients seven years ago."

"I think so. I don't remember for sure, but what about them?" Mom often comes home with stories from work.

"They're the nicest family—always making small talk while I'm there, and today, we were chatting about our kids, and I happened to mention that you finished your senior year early and needed a full-time job until fall, and guess what?" she asks, beaming. Her excitement is contagious, making me smile.

"What?"

"Well, their son, Jackson, who was already out of the house when I started for them, took over their property management company when they retired—Soloman Management or something. Their daughter, Cici, was supposed to run it with him but ended up moving away. I remember when she lived at home, she was such a sweetheart. I can't believe she left."

"Mom! Get to the point. What's the good news?" I interrupt her rambling, growing impatient. She tends to do this, drone on and on, taking forever to finish her stories. I'm honestly surprised to hear that the Solomans talk with her so much. My mom can be overwhelming at times. God bless her.

"Well, they mentioned that Jackson's assistant is going on maternity leave and that they needed a temporary replacement. I told them how smart and mature you are, graduating from high school early with all those advanced classes, and I can't believe it, but they offered you the job!"

"Like, they want me to interview for it?" This might be perfect, and I bet it would pay decent money.

She has the biggest smile on her face. "No, honey, they want you to start training on Monday. No interview necessary. They said any daughter of mine will be amazing, and with the drive you're showing, you'll be great."

I'm stunned. "Monday? Wow… that's just… wow…"

"That's good, right? I figured you needed something to do anyway since you won't have school anymore. Maybe it'll go so well that they keep you on until you start college in the fall." She's so happy, it's infectious.

My plan was to continue playing poker, but this way, I could make money guilt-free. Maybe it'll also give me time for a social life. If I work eight to five, I can go out at night like most people my age instead of playing tournaments. I'd still make meals and help around the house, but with my nights and weekends free, I'd have plenty of time for everything.

"It's great, Mom… just crazy that I start on Monday with no interview, but with the timing, it's like it was meant to be. They know I have no office experience, though, right?" The doubt is seeping in.

"Sweetheart, you'll do great. I'm sure you'll pick it up in no time. You have nothing to worry about with how smart and re-sponsible you are. Why don't you go up to start picking your out-fits for next week and let me clean up."

"Mom, you worked all day. I can do it. I have all weekend to decide what to wear, but nice try. You should take a bath and relax. I don't mind." I refuse to let her clean when she gets home.

"Mia, I don't know what I did to deserve you, but I sure am lucky. I love you, honey. Come say good night when you're done."

"All right, I'll be up in a few."

I ruminate over my new job while putting away dinner and ti-dying up the kitchen. I'll be an assistant to the owner—well, the owner's son. I know nothing about him or Soloman Management, so I'll have to do some research over the weekend. The last thing I want is to walk in unprepared and clueless.

After saying one more thank you and final good night to Mom, I rush to get ready for bed so I can call my best friend, Walker, and tell him the good news. He knows how much it bothers me to lie about the extra income. Another positive is that I'll have something to keep me busy during the day since, unlike me, he's still in school until graduation.

I'm a nervous wreck getting ready for my first day. I played my last poker games over the weekend, even declining an invite to a live tournament this week. Since I'm taking this job, I've decided to go legit. Being full-time should cover the extra expenses I take care of and still allow me to save for a car. Poker is lucrative, so it's hard to give up, but knowing how upset Mom would be if she knew is enough motivation to quit.

Pairing my classiest black skirt with a fitted purple ribbed V-neck is the best I came up with from my limited selection. Clothes have been at the bottom of my list for the past few years. Gold hoop earrings complete the look with my favorite necklace, a nightingale spreading its wings. It was a graduation present from my mom, a tribute to my middle name, which happens to be Nightingale. Finishing up with two sprays of my favorite scent and my only pair of heels, a wedge sandal, I'm as ready as I can be for a first impression.

I enter the kitchen but don't dare eat with the butterflies in my stomach. Puking at work on day one is not on my to-do list. Instead, I grab a cup of coffee and try to stay calm.

"You look great, sweetie. Are you excited?" My mom appears from around the corner.

"More nervous, but what are you still doing here? I thought you had a job at seven."

"I couldn't miss my baby's first day of work. I'll just be home an hour later tonight. Do you want to order pizza for dinner since we'll probably both be tired?"

"That's perfect. Sorry you have to work late, but I'm glad you're here now. What do you think?" I spin around.

"Very professional. I can't believe how grown-up you look. You're going to do amazing. I know it. Be confident and remember how wonderful you are, mija." She leans in to hug me.

"I love you, Mom. Thanks again for getting me this job."

"Of course. You're going to have a great first day. I can't wait to hear all about it," she says before grabbing her things and heading out the door.

After a few more minutes, I force myself to follow and make my way to the bus. It's not a long commute, but it's enough to ponder all my research from the weekend. I learned that Soloman Management Group is a pretty big deal. They not only do property management for numerous places but own many of the buildings they manage. Even more impressive is that they started from nothing and grew their business to become one of the largest in southern California.

I tried to look up Jackson but only saw his business profile and some family bio regarding their company. I found an article that said Mr. and Mrs. Soloman retired, entrusting their son, Jackson, to carry on, but that sums it up. He exists on Instagram but hasn't posted in years, so he's not on social media much. I couldn't find anything else regarding Jackson or the company. From the few old pictures I did see, he's hot. But being that he's a decade older, attraction shouldn't be an issue.

From the sidewalk, I study the building before me. It's not pretentious, just an ordinary, one-level office building. It's large, though, with only one sign above the main entrance, indicating they occupy the whole thing. With as many buildings in their portfolio, it makes sense that they need ample space.

Taking a deep breath, I walk in and see a large reception desk. "Hi, I'm Mia Marcos. I start training today as the temporary assistant for Jackson Soloman."

"Oh yeah, great. Let's start with your paperwork, and then I'll take you back to Cindy." She hands me a clipboard and directs me to the chairs. "Have a seat and take your time. Come see me when you're done."

My nerves are skyrocketing as I fill out the forms with shaky hands. Once I'm finished, my palms sweat as I'm led back to meet Jackson's current assistant, Cindy. Her desk is in an open area toward the back corner of the building with a large office behind it. The office, which I assume is Jackson's, has two massive windows on each side of the closed door with blinds that are shut, preventing a glimpse of my new boss.

When Cindy stands to greet me, my eyes immediately gravitate to her protruding belly. I can't believe she's still working.

"Mia, I'm so happy to meet you. I was excited when Hazel called to tell me you'd be training. You'll be a perfect fit while I'm gone."

"Thanks. I, uh, well, I'll just be upfront and tell you I have no experience, but I'm a fast learner." She's still standing, and I wonder how she's managing. "Please, sit down. I feel like you could have a baby any minute." *Crap, did I say that out loud?*

She laughs. "I wish, but I still have six weeks. It looks worse than it is, I promise. It's all the popcorn and chocolate over the last seven months. Advice for the future: Don't use pregnancy as an excuse to eat whatever you want. It doesn't work out in the end."

I like her already. Laughing, I respond, "I'll try to remember that in about ten years. But seriously, let's sit down." A chair has already been placed beside hers, so we both take a seat.

She shows me how to do some morning tasks, supervising while I work. The next time I glance at the clock, I see we've been at it for a couple of hours already, and things are going great. She'd prepared everything for an easy transition.

While we wait for a program to boot up, I take the opportunity to ask about the boss. "So… what's Jackson like? I tried to do some research, but nothing came up."

Instead of answering, I see her eyes dart past my shoulder.

"Good to know my new assistant is cyberstalking me," comes a deep voice from behind.

Seriously? The man is stealthy.

I swivel in my chair to get my first look at Jackson, towering behind me with a scowl. That answers one question—not so warm and fuzzy, then. But, wow, the last few years have been good to him. He's built like a beast and could probably snap me in half. Does he live at the gym or what? I mean, seriously, his muscles look like they're about to bust the seams of his long-sleeved dress shirt. After you get past his biceps, those bright blue eyes draw you in immediately. But it's his casually styled blond hair hanging slightly over his forehead that gives him a boyish charm. He's gorgeous, even with the asshole vibes he's radiating.

"I… I was trying to research the company I'd be working for. My mom didn't give much information besides the business name and the fact that the owners are nice."

For some reason, that earns me another scowl. I can tell he's going to be tough to win over.

"Yeah, they're the nicest. I'll be in my office. Message me if you need anything, Cindy. Good luck." With that, he walks straight into his office and slams the door.

Okay, he's not happy I'm here. Which is rude, considering he doesn't even know me. Screw him.

Although he is my boss, so I'd like to start off on the right foot.

"So… I feel like that wasn't a great first impression." I look to Cindy for advice.

"He's usually a softy, but he's under a lot of stress lately with all our restructuring. Why don't you try that again and introduce yourself properly? Maybe offer to get him some coffee." She gives me a look of encouragement as I stand.

Pulling my skirt down and smoothing my shirt, I rap lightly on the door before entering. Walking forward with slow, unsure steps, I approach his desk while he stares with venom.

Whoa, talk about intimidating. Strangely, it's kind of sexy, which hits me out of nowhere and is so out of character.

"Um, I just wanted to introduce myself and thank you properly. I'm Mia, and I'm truly grateful for the opportunity to be here and eager to learn. I'm prepared to do whatever it takes, sir."

Could that have sounded any worse?

Jackson

I peruse her up and down in silence, and what I see is unexpected. Her thick black hair is pulled back, showcasing her slim neckline and gorgeous face. Her darker skin tone is attractive; I remember it was mentioned that her mom is Puerto Rican. It's her large round eyes that do it, though. They're soft and innocent, with defiance lurking just beneath the surface. She's stunning is what she is, which only pisses me off more. But apparently, she is eager to learn.

It must be my lucky day.

"You're eager to learn, huh? Well, here's your first lesson. Knock and wait until I answer before you step into my office. And don't thank me. Thank my parents. You wouldn't be here if it were up to me, little girl. Now... Mia, is it?" She nods in stunned silence. "Get out and shut the door behind you."

Her jaw drops. Usually, I'd take that open mouth as an invitation. Unfortunately, she's off the table unless I want to be in cuffs.

Finally coming out of her stupor, she swivels and tries to walk out calmly with all the dignity she can muster. She gets props for keeping it together... she might be more of a challenge than I thought. Still, I give her a week—tops.

On the other hand, I could certainly get used to the view she gives me on the way out. That's the finest ass I've seen in a while, plump and perfect on her slim little frame. I could do some damage to that body of hers, that's for sure.

Fuuuuck. What am I thinking? I cannot possibly be attracted to a girl her age.

This week is going to be long as fuck.

My door opens once again, and Cindy comes barreling

toward my desk. "What did you say to her? She was white as a ghost when she came out."

"Only the truth. She wouldn't be here if my parents hadn't insisted. She's seventeen, Cindy. There's no way she's qualified to fill your shoes."

"You don't know that. I can already tell she has a good head on her shoulders. You were young once, remember? Did you like being treated like a child? At least give her a chance, Jackson. You've scared the crap out of her, and I won't always be here to run interference."

Cindy is the only reason my head stays above water. She's been my right hand ever since I started full-time after college. She deals with my excessive demands and doesn't complain about my blunt communication skills. She also puts up with random office visits from my flavors of the month. I would have paid her not to have kids had I known I'd be without her for so long. She asked to be home with the baby for the first six months, and it wasn't difficult to acquiesce rather than risk losing her for good.

"Look, she won't last the week. Don't worry. We'll find someone else for you to train before it's too late. Just indulge her for now, but don't waste much effort."

"We'll see about that. She might surprise you, you know. In the meantime, be nicer. She's darling, and I think she'll work out great if you let her." Cindy always sees the good in people, that's for sure.

"I'll leave her alone for the rest of the day. Satisfied?"

"It'll do for now." She leaves, closing the door behind her.

Damn, that woman is relentless sometimes. It sounds like she's already got a soft spot for the girl. That didn't take long.

It puts a damper on my plan, but I'll figure something out.

That girl cannot walk around here for the next eight months, that's for sure. She's way too fucking tempting. Although, I wonder if she enjoys an occasional hookup.

For Christ's sake, what am I thinking? She might not even have *hooked up* yet. Nah, no way. Kids are doing it early these days. Fuck, I'm going down a rabbit hole.

On that note, I grab my phone to respond to Jessica, last weekend's conquest. She texted me this morning that she'd love to stop by and say hi. The eggplant emoji was all I needed to know her intention. She couldn't have picked a better day. Satisfied that she's on her way, I distract myself with work while impatiently waiting.

It's not long before the phone intercom beeps. "There's a Jessica here to see you, sir."

Damn Cindy for having Mia make the announcement. She's the last thing I need on my mind right now.

"Send her in," I reply curtly before a soft "Yes, sir" sounds in reply.

Fuck. Me.

It's hard and over quickly, just the way I needed it, and judging from her eagerness, she did too.

Alone once more, I drop my head into my hands, feeling no better than I did fifteen minutes ago. I cannot believe I just fucked a woman while imagining she was my new, hot little assistant. What the hell is wrong with me? Mia is a child—I should not be fantasizing about her. Women have always been a weakness, but this is a new low. I need to get out of here, stat.

After hitting the gym for a couple of hours, I call it a day because there's no convincing myself to return to the office. Having already texted Eli and Braden, I head to the bar where we meet when it's too early for the club scene.

There's no traffic this afternoon, so getting there takes minutes. I spot them immediately and make my way over, feeling the tension I've been holding begin to release.

"Hey, guys. Thanks for meeting so early. I needed out of the office." I run my hand down my face and blow the air from my lungs, grateful to see a beer waiting for me.

"She's that bad, huh?" Braden knows why I'm on edge, having heard about it over the weekend.

"She's that hot is more like it. I wasn't expecting her to be total eye candy. I can't have her running around there, tempting me with those fucking curves. Especially not when she's a minor, for fuck's sake." I won't be able to handle it.

"Whoa, whoa, whoa, back up. You're lusting over a kid?" This from Eli, who's not been clued in.

So, I bring him up to date.

"That's fucked up. When does she turn eighteen?" Eli might be more of a womanizer than I am if that question is any indication.

"Dude, she's almost a decade younger. That's a lifetime at our age. It's not happening. She's a baby, for fuck's sake," I say.

"Doesn't sound like a baby if she gets your dick hard, dude. Plus, girls have always matured faster than us, so maybe you two are on the same level," Braden says, laughing.

Fucking Braden.

"A couple of months," I say, ignoring him and answering Eli's question. "It was the first thing I looked at after she left my office. There's no way I can go two months with that ass parading around my office and not fuck up."

My beer is already empty. Signaling the server for another, I sigh, exasperated.

"Well, it sounds like you're gonna have to. Hopefully, you have someone to keep you occupied. If not, it'll be a long couple of months, buddy." Braden, ever the realist.

I raise my refilled glass in a toast. "Then here's to keeping myself sufficiently occupied."

$\mathcal{2}$

GAME ON

Jackson

THE REST OF THE WEEK GOES NO BETTER. I'M ANGRY AND SICK of hiding in my office to avoid the brat and bear witness to any more of Cindy's fawning over the girl. I've been as cruel as possible without earning more tongue-lashing from Cindy, who seems to like Mia more than she does me. I can't blame her with the mood I've been in.

However, my tactics aren't working—I've produced no tears and no snarky attitude by the end of the week, thus giving me no reason to write her up. Moreover, she hasn't quit. She doesn't even seem bothered by my demeanor and continues to lay on the eager employee act. There's no way she can be this unaffected; she's either oblivious to moods around her, or she's a damn good actress. I'm going with the latter, which means I'm not giving up. I'll break her down eventually.

In the meantime, I have the weekend to regroup, decompress, and deliberate how to up my game. I'm planning to get my fill in the bedroom over the next couple of days, so maybe I'll stop fantasizing about taking Mia over my desk every time she walks in.

Speaking of… "Come in," I say after the second knock on my office door—because why would I make it easy on her? And I know it's her because Cindy doesn't knock.

"Did you need anything else handled before the weekend, sir?" I'm sure Cindy put her up to this. She still thinks I'll come around eventually and be nice to the girl. She couldn't be further from the truth. In fact, an idea just popped into my head.

"I do, but it requires your services over the weekend. Our cleaning company had something come up and can't make their usual rounds to clean the common areas. I'll need you to handle that," I tell her curtly without further instruction. The longer I draw it out, the more reaction I expect to get.

"Do you need me to call and find a replacement company for the weekend?" she asks as she writes on her notepad, trying not to make eye contact.

"No, as in, you need to do it yourself. Your mom is a house cleaner, right? This shouldn't be much of a stretch for you." With that comment, I see the slightest tic of her jaw—finally, something.

"You want me to clean over the weekend?" She looks a little taken aback. This is more fun than anticipated.

"I expect you to do your job, and right now, that entails handling a problem by whatever means necessary. Are you unwilling to perform the duties required?" I sit back in my chair and thread my fingers behind my head.

"How many buildings need to be cleaned? Will I be paid

overtime?" At least she's got a head on her shoulders to consider that.

"Does this look like the payroll department? You can direct your questions there. I'll have maintenance provide you with a list of buildings, locations, and requirements for each one. That's all."

She pastes on the biggest smile before saying, "Great, I'll get it done, sir. See you Monday."

On her way out the door, I get the last word in. "Enjoy your weekend, Mia."

She doesn't turn around, and I'd give anything to see the eye roll I'm sure she did.

When the door closes, I pick up my phone and dial maintenance. "Hey, buddy, it's Jackson. I need you to do something for me. I'm having Mia, my assistant in training, clean our buildings this weekend to familiarize herself with our properties. Can you print off the cleaning schedule and task list we provide our crew and get it to her? Let the team know they have the weekend off, and I'll pay as scheduled."

"Can do. I'm sure they'll appreciate it. Thanks, boss."

"You bet. Have a good weekend and say hi to the missus."

"Will do."

Okay, that felt way too good. It's my first genuine smile all week. Who knew being an asshole could be so much fun. I think it calls for a celebration.

> Me: Club tonight?

> Braden: Does someone have some pent-up sexual tension?

> Eli: How many times have you jacked off this week?

> Me: Fuck off. I'll see you bastards later, and I won't be jerking off tonight.

Mia

What a prick. It's not the request that bothers me, it's the fricking delivery. Other than not going out with Walker and Ben tonight, I'm not upset about it. And hopefully, I'll be getting paid extra. It sucks that I'll have to tell my mom another white lie in addition to the ones I've been feeding her all week about how great my boss is. If I were to say what my job was this weekend, she'd insist on helping, and that's not happening. I'll use Walker as my cover and say I'm hanging at his place since that's what used to happen before he got serious with Ben.

"How did it go in there? He didn't give you a hard time, did he?" Cindy has been a godsend this week. Things could have been worse if she hadn't stepped in to defend me. She's become my haven and the only bright spot in this place. I don't know what I'll do when she's gone. Luckily, I still have plenty of time.

"He was as pleasant as always. The cleaning company had some emergency, so I'm cleaning the buildings over the weekend. I could use the extra cash anyway." What sucks is that I'm using public transportation between each building. It's going to be a long weekend.

"That's unfortunate. I hope it didn't ruin any big plans you had." Cindy makes up for Jackson's rudeness.

My email pings, and I see that the information has arrived. I open the file as I answer. "No, nothing important. I'm here to learn and make money, so it's fine. But looking at this list, I think it might take all weekend. Do you mind if I cut out now and get a head start?"

"Not at all. I'll see you Monday, Mia."

"Thanks. See you next week." I wave before walking away.

I'm out the door after a quick stop in payroll to ask about weekend hours. Reading the instructions as I go, I'm relieved to see that each location has its own supply closet with supplies. Good thing I didn't wear a skirt today, so I can hit a few of these on my way home.

It's a perfect time to call Walker en route to the first stop.

"How was the asshat today?" he answers with no pretenses. Walker has been my outlet all week. I usually have most of it out of my system when Mom comes home, thanks to him.

"Miserable as usual, if not more. You'd think it would be getting better by now, but I swear it seems to be going in the opposite direction, especially after this. He gave me extra work over the weekend, so I won't be able to go with you guys tonight." I'm expecting an argument.

"Bullshit. What did he ask you to do, take notes while he jerks off staring at your chest?"

"Ew, gross. He doesn't stare at my chest." Not that I'd know because I try not to make eye contact. "He thinks I'm a child, not to mention despises me. Anyway, I'm cleaning some of the buildings they manage. Their cleaning crew couldn't make it for some reason."

"So now you're his personal bitch. It's getting worse, Mia. And just so you know, he's male. All males think you're gorgeous and stare at your chest. It's the nature of the beast. Also, I hate to break it to you, but your age does not prohibit your boss from having dirty thoughts about you."

"Gee, thanks for putting that in my head."

"That's what friends are for. Now, why are you putting up with this crap? And more importantly, why can't you come tonight? You have all day tomorrow and Sunday to clean if you insist on doing his dirty work." Walker wouldn't know what it's like to need a job and the money that goes with it because it grows on trees in his family. It's never been an issue with us, but he doesn't always get it.

"Walker, I love you, but we've talked about this. I need the money, and my mom got me this job. It means a lot to her, and I want to prove I can do it. I won't let some bosshole scare me away from a good job. He may be the first one I have to deal with, but I'm sure he won't be the last, so I might as well learn how to handle it now."

"You're probably right, but remember, there are other jobs out there. Anyway, what about tonight? Come with us, and I'll help you for half the day tomorrow—the second half once my hangover goes away."

"In that case, fine. Pick me up on your way. Also, I'm staying over this weekend. I don't want my mom to know I'm working." Thank goodness I have Walker for things like this.

"You got it. I'll see you tonight."

Before he can hang up, I shout, "I'm holding you to helping me tomorrow!" It'll be nice having a ride for part of it. And I miss spending time with my best friend.

I'm glad Walker made me go out with them last night. He was right; I had fun, and it was seriously needed after the week from hell. But I'm currently paying the price. I wish I had the luxury of staying in bed half the day and nursing my hangover like Walker, but duty calls, which means I'm dealing with the headache from hell as I work.

While dusting an area of the lobby in the current building, I hear someone enter, stopping behind me instead of proceeding to the elevator, raising my hackles. Turning around, I see my least favorite person on the planet.

"Did you come to check up on me?" I ask the man responsible for my presence.

"I live here, but glad to see you're following orders."

"I aim to please, sir." I give him my megawatt smile through gritted teeth when a sudden sharp head pain makes me wince.

"Are you okay?" he asks, concern lacing his voice.

"Yeah, I'm fine. Just one drink too many last night."

"You're way too young to be drinking."

Seriously? He's going to lecture me about my private life?

"Right, and I'm sure you never drank at this age. You don't strike me as the golden child." I shouldn't engage, but I can't help it.

"Oh yeah? What type do I strike you as then?"

Damn, it's hard focusing on the conversation when his muscular bronze chest, on display from a few undone buttons, is right in front of my eyes due to his considerable height.

"The wild child who started drinking and having sex in middle school. Rebellious, defiant, and still hasn't grown out of it."

"That's quite the assessment. And you derived all this how?" His left eyebrow rises.

"Well, you don't like that your parents gave me this job, thus defiant, and you're acting rebellious by treating me like shit. You had some skank come to your office for sex, so I'm assuming you've been around the block. As for the drinking, I suppose it goes with everything else. How did I do?" I ask, cocking my head to the side and wincing again from another shooting head pain.

"I guess you've got me all figured out. Not to step outside the box, but do you need some medicine for your headache?"

I just got whiplash.

Shaking my head, I respond, "Uh, no. I already took some. I'm just waiting for them to set in. Thanks, though."

"All right, I'll let you get back to work. Bye, Mia."

"See you Monday," I say with a smile as he walks into the elevator, then immediately drop it and sigh in relief when the doors shut.

I was doing such a good job of hiding how much he gets under my skin, but it's exhausting, and I don't have the energy this morning. I can't believe I said all that, but dammit if he didn't egg me on with the jab about my age. And what was with his nonengagement? He didn't even argue, so maybe I was spot on.

He lives in a nice place, that's for sure. So far, this is the swankiest building I've been in. Judging from his clothes, it looks like he didn't stay here last night, and I can't help but wonder if he was with the girl who visited the office or if he has a different one for each day of the week.

Ugh, who cares? It's not my concern and nothing I should be thinking about anyway. But dang, it's hard not to when he looks so good. His blond hair was casually messed up from an obvious overnighter, and as always, I could see the contour of his thick muscular arms under the shirt. A tiny part of me wonders what it would feel like to have them wrapped around me. And that's what occupies my thoughts the rest of the day.

That was seriously one of the most exhausting weekends of my life. But being familiar with their properties will be good for the job, so

I suppose it was worth it. I'm just glad Walker came through; otherwise, finishing would have been a stretch. I don't know how my mom has done it all these years. Thank goodness for the full scholarship to San Diego State because I don't have it in me to follow in her footsteps.

After this weekend and last week's training, I'd be fine taking over now if I had to. Cindy did a great job getting things ready for her to leave. The situation with Jackson, however, needs improvement. He's beyond rude and practically refuses to deal with me, talking to Cindy like I'm not even present most of the time. His plan to get me to quit last week was obvious, but he doesn't know how stubborn I am. Plus, I'm familiar with chauvinistic assholes like him from the poker table, and I love winning while being underestimated.

I'm surprised Cindy isn't in when I get to her desk. Instead of twiddling my thumbs while I wait, I get right to it, working down the list she made. She had the foresight to create a spreadsheet with staff names, their corresponding departments, and responsibilities, along with daily tasks. I've gone through voicemails, returned a few calls, made a couple of appointments, and printed out today's agenda all by the time Jackson walks in. When I look up, I forget for a moment what a complete ass he is. As far as looks go, he takes the cake. If only he had the personality to go with it.

Pasting on a smile, I greet him with as much enthusiasm as possible. "Good morning, sir. Do you need anything right away, or would you like me to go over the agenda for today?"

"Cut the crap. Where's Cindy?"

Aaand we're off to a great start.

"She hasn't arrived yet, so I dove right in. Does she have the day off?" I ask.

"No, she doesn't have the day off. Fuck… just… keep doing

whatever you're doing. I'll figure it out." He stomps into his office and slams the door.

Okay then… that went well. Cue eyeroll.

I continue with the voicemails from the weekend. Everyone and their dog must decide to call after hours so they don't have to speak to an actual person. Most people want to be rude and complain to a machine so they won't get talked back to. Luckily, most everything is delegated to other departments in the company—it's just a matter of getting it to the right person.

I've finally run out of things I can do on my own and, unfortunately, need Jackson's assistance with the rest. I have no choice but to ask for guidance on things requiring his attention. I'm not looking forward to interacting with the bosshole, but it's a necessary evil. I'll have to fake it 'til I make it.

This should be fun.

I pause outside the door, remembering his warning from my first day, and knock lightly. Nothing. I knock again. Nothing. By the third attempt, I pound on the door, earning me a curt reply to enter. Bracing myself, I stand tall and straighten my shoulders before opening the door. He doesn't even look up while typing away.

"What?" he asks gruffly while still not looking at me. At least he knows I'm here.

"I've finished with everything I can from this morning," I say as I walk toward the desk. "Here's a list of items that require your review, along with today's agenda. Is there anything you need me for, sir?"

He finally looks up with a smirk before shaking his head like he remembered his rule of only scowling at me.

"What do you mean, you've finished everything? Do you even know how to use the computer?" His tone is as condescending as can be.

This week is shaping up to be no different than the last. I think it's time to give him a taste of his own medicine. I'm done backing down. "You might be too old to know this, but we use computers in high school these days, and I was already familiar with most of the programs Cindy showed me." The look on his face is furious. Oh well, nothing new. "Where is Cindy, by the way?"

"She unexpectedly went into labor this morning, and I just found out. She and the baby are doing well, but she's officially on maternity leave starting today. That means you're on your own. Can you handle it, or should I make other arrangements?"

Oh, wouldn't that make his day. Sorry to disappoint—not. "I can handle whatever you give me." It takes all my willpower not to be snarky now that I'm taking the gloves off, but I decide it's not worth getting fired on my first day without Cindy.

"I highly doubt that, but challenge accepted. For now, just answer the phone. I'll let you know when I need you."

Asshole. Damn that he's such a handsome one.

He won't need me, as he clearly thinks I'm an imbecile. Now, if he needed me in other ways…

Oh my God, where did that come from? I cannot fantasize about my boss. I swear it's Walker's fault for putting thoughts in my head.

Jackson

Challenge accepted? When I need you? Where the fuck is my head at?

The answer is obvious but highly inappropriate. She's in another formfitting skirt today that hugs her voluptuous ass that I can't get enough of. Why I don't call her in more often just to watch her walk away is a shame. Then there's the low-cut shirt that cuts right across the top of her breasts. With the words that come from her mouth along with that body, she's killing me. My dirty thoughts shot through the roof when she asked if I needed her for anything. *Fuck yeah, I need you to bend over my desk and give me a better look.*

I grab the back of my neck and forcefully blow out air. I've got to get my mind out of the gutter. There's no fucking way this is going to work. Picking up the phone, I dial my parents.

"Hi, honey. To what do we owe the pleasure?" Mom answers. I can tell I'm on speaker.

"Cindy had her baby this morning. They're both doing well, but because it was early, they'll need to stay in the hospital for a couple of weeks. I told her I'd give her a few days before visiting."

"That's great news, son. Thanks for letting us know. We'll be sure to send our congratulations," Dad says from the background.

"The bad news is that I now have an assistant with one week of training and no clue what she's doing. I want to bring someone in from a temp agency." This favor they made without my involvement pisses me off.

Apparently, Dad had a sip of the Mia Kool-Aid, judging by his response. "Jackson, we made a commitment. It may be tough for a few days, but she'll catch on. Look at the positive. This way, you can teach her the ropes and show her exactly how you want things."

And my mind is right back in the gutter. "How do you not see that I need someone with more experience? It's a busy time for the company. She's too young to keep up." And too young for me to be in lust with.

"We're done with this conversation, Jackson. Mia is your new assistant, and you'll have to accept that. Make it work. Cindy will be back before you know it." Mom's final words.

Fuck, why did I even try?

Me: Cindy went into labor today. My parents won't let me get rid of the girl. What the fuck am I supposed to do?

Braden: Jerk off…

Eli: Give her a birthday present she'll remember… in two months.

Braden: A lot…

Me: Assholes.

Eli: There's a cash game this Friday. You guys in? It'll be a good distraction.

Me: Yeah, I'm in. Send me the info.

Braden: Next time. I have a date.

Me: Sucker.

Braden: I hope she is. At least I'm not using my hand. Good luck with that.

Me: Fuck you.

I can't avoid her forever; I need a fucking assistant. "We need to go over a few things. Come in and plan to take notes," I say over the intercom.

She answers with her typical response. "Yes, sir."

Sighing in frustration, I run a hand through my hair. If I don't solve this problem, it's going to be a long six months.

She enters seconds later.

"Have a seat." She doesn't look afraid. I keep underestimating her. She seems to have nerves of steel, or she's damn good at hiding fear. Either way, it's time to move forward.

"I'm sure it's apparent that I'm less than thrilled to have you here. No offense, but you're young, and you lack experience. If it weren't for my parents, you'd already be gone. That being said, we have to make this work for now. Cindy must've done a good job training you last week since you've managed this far into the day without her."

"She had me do everything with minimal assistance. She also created a company directory and a list of daily tasks. If you give me a chance, I'll prove I'm not too young for this. I can do the job, I swear. Since you seem pretty hung up on my age, you'll be happy to know I'll be eighteen soon. Then you can stop treating me like a child."

Sweetheart, if you knew why your age is a problem for me, you might not want your birthday to come so soon.

I narrow my eyes at her. "I'll stop treating you like a child when I see proof that you aren't one. Until then, just do your job."

"Will do, sir." Her face is earnest.

Fuck, if this is going to work, I need to set some ground rules.

"You need to stop calling me sir. I'm not fifty."

"Would you prefer Mr. Soloman?"

"I'm also not my dad. Just use my name."

"Okay… Jackson."

Hearing my name from her lips gives me an unexpected desire to hear it more, wondering what it would sound like while she's begging for my dick. *Fuuuuck.*

"And you need to start wearing more appropriate clothing," I add, frustrated at my drifting thoughts.

"What's wrong with my clothes?" She looks affronted. Shit. Why did she pick today to let her guard down? I can't tell her to wear sweats to work. I just pinned myself up against a wall.

"Nothing, never mind."

"What? Are they not expensive enough to be acceptable? Sorry, I don't shop in designer stores like you." She's offended, which wasn't what I meant to do. "At least I'm not in rags."

I'm not fast enough to stop my next words from tumbling out. "I'd rather you be in rags," I mutter.

"What is that supposed to mean?" She doesn't get it at all; that's how naïve she is.

"I said never mind. Forget I mentioned anything."

"No, tell me. I need to know if there's some sort of dress code around here." She's not going to let this go.

"Fuck. You want an explanation? Here it is. I meant that I'd rather you walk around in sweats than have you tempting me while you're completely off-limits. Is that clear enough for you, little girl?" Goddammit. Did I just admit my attraction to her? I watch as her face goes red, and that alone makes my confession worth it.

"Oh… okay… I'll take that into consideration." She pauses and then continues with an adorable pout on her face. "And I am not a child, so stop referring to me like one." Of course that's what has her irritated over all else.

"You are until your age says otherwise." She rolls her eyes, proving that she's done pretending to be immune to my attitude, which might make this situation a little more entertaining if nothing else. "Moving on. Order flowers to be delivered to Cindy's room at the hospital—no price limit. Go extravagant, and I'll email you what to put on the card. Also, get an update from our attorneys on the Bryer Building and Delaware transaction. That's it for now. You can go."

"Thank you, sir… I mean Jackson." She didn't even try hiding that she did that on purpose. This damn girl is playing with fire.

I watch her strut out of the office, and I swear she has a little more sway to her hips—fucking tease. My situation just became a lot more complicated. Shit.

Needing a distraction, I pick up the phone and dial my sister,

Cici, as soon as the door shuts. She answers on the second ring. "Hey, Jackson!" It's good to hear her voice.

"I just want you to know I'm still pissed at you for leaving, and with the latest development, I'm never forgiving you," I tell her.

"What's got you so cranky?"

I catch her up on the situation.

"Okay, well, how is she doing so far?"

"She's been here a week. Who the fuck knows? Today's the first day she's been on her own, and I've been dealing with the weekend's bullshit all morning, not paying attention to what she's doing." Not completely true; I've been paying plenty of attention to her sweet ass as it exits my office each time. Okay—and I'll admit this to no one—she did handle the morning way better than I expected and *maybe* knows what she's doing.

"Snap out of it and figure shit out. She's there, so you might as well use her." She lectures.

Fuck, everything sounds like an innuendo about Mia right now. That's the main problem, one I'm not sharing with Cici.

"Did you not hear me? She's a high school student. There's no way she should be taking over Cindy's job. I'm so fucking frustrated."

"I get it, Jackson. But just because Mom and Dad are digging their heels in doesn't make it this girl's fault. What's her name?" It comes out of my lips with venom before she continues. "It's not Mia's fault you're in this position, so don't take it out on her. Trust me, I know what you can be like when you're mad. Be nice. At least it's only temporary, right?" She knows how it is when our parents make demands, but that doesn't mean she gets this particular situation.

"Easy for you to say, runner."

"Yeah, yeah. Miss you too. Keep me posted. And seriously, *be nice.*"

I chuckle as I hang up the phone after we say goodbye. I love my sister, and I get why she left, but I'm not going to stop giving her shit for it, even though I'm proud of her. She never liked being under our parents' control and knew early on that she wanted to make her own way, even though doing so got her cut off. It took balls for her to leave, but she's thriving now, and unbeknownst to her, I check on her frequently. I can't say I'd have made the same decision if this wasn't what I wanted to do, but luckily it is.

She wants me to be nice to Mia, but if that happens, we'll have a different problem altogether. Better stick with the plan.

Visit www.bethanyrosa.com to purchase your copy of *Dangerous Pursuit*

Or simply scan below:

If you'd like to purchase other books in the Pursuit Series or keep up with upcoming releases and learn more about author Bethany Rosa, visit www.BethanyRosa.com

Or scan below: